DEBBIE THO...

CLASS ACT

MERCIER PRESS
IRISH PUBLISHER – IRISH STORY

For Grand Pat and Lovely Boy

MERCIER PRESS

Cork

www.mercierpress.ie

© Debbie Thomas, 2015
Cover illustration by Stella Macdonald

ISBN: 978 1 78117 262 9
10 9 8 7 6 5 4 3 2 1

Printed and bound in the EU.

CONTENTS

Chapter 1

POINTLESS

Have you ever wondered what's the point of you?

I bet you haven't. I bet you've never woken up thinking, *Why am I here again? There must be a reason but it's slipped my mind.*

And even if you have, I bet your parents soon told you. I bet, as you wandered down to breakfast, they said, 'Oh, there you are, Michelangelo,' or whatever your name is. 'What a relief you're here to fill our lives with joy and meaning. Have some Coco Pops.'

And even if they didn't, I bet your friends put things straight. I bet, as you skipped into school, they cried, 'Hey, Fantastica,' or whatever you're called, 'thank goodness you've arrived. Today was a waste of time until you came in to make our hearts do handstands and our souls play the banjo.'

And even if they forgot, I bet your teacher didn't. I bet he or she or it (it can be hard to tell) looked up and gasped, 'Oh, Chardonnay de Twinklehoops, what *would* I have

7

done if you hadn't come, bringing eternal loveliness and the smell of fresh muffins into the classroom?'

Unless you're Brian O'Bunion. In which case the bet's off.

No one said those things to him. Not ever. Not even on cloudless Thursdays in August when the birds sang and ants played poker on the lawn.

Why would they? His teacher hated him. He had no school friends. And his dad had forgotten to buy Coco Pops for two years, one month and nineteen days.

'What about his mum?' you might ask. Well please don't, because for the last two years, one month and nineteen days she hadn't been to the shops. Or the hairdresser. Or the dentist or the school gates or even the kitchen.

The only place she *had* visited was Brian's dream: the one he had whenever he felt worried or sad or scared. The one he'd had just now.

She'd been smiling down at him. Her face sparkled, as if a bucket of sunlight had been poured over her head. Her brown eyes creased at the edges. She opened her mouth in a grin – no a grimace – and now the creases were spreading, racing across her face like cracks across ice. Her cheeks splintered, her nose shattered. And then she was gone.

Brian sat up in bed. He drew up his knees and hugged the duvet, blinking in the sunlight that blazed through a gap in the curtains. The day rolled out before him like a mouldy carpet. June the ninth: the second worst day of the year, topped – or rather bottomed – by April the twentieth, anniversary of the Great Unspeakable. Today was the day when his pointlessness would shine for the whole world to see, if it could be bothered to look.

The school prize-giving always took place on the second Monday in June. And the last time Brian had won anything was … hang on, let's check, I'm sure I made a note of it. Ah yes, there we are … never. In eight years at Tullybun Primary he was the only pupil not to have won a thing. That in itself was quite an achievement because there were prizes for practically everything. Beyond the usual stuff – brains and sporting talent – there were awards for:

Neatest Handwriting
Tidiest Desk
Calmest Walking in Corridor
Most Opening of Doors for Teachers
Coolest Lunch Box
Cleanest Socks – teachers did random smell checks –

and

Most Popular Pupil – children handed in every party invitation they received over the year and the teacher put a tick by their name on a big bright chart on the classroom wall.

The list went on. But Brian wouldn't be on it. His handwriting looked like cartwheeling ants. He brought his lunch in an old ice-cream box. And the number of invitation ticks by his name was … hold on, let's see. I know I wrote it down somewhere. Yes, there we go … none.

Brian reached over and drew back the curtains. That didn't help. The sky was blue, for goodness sake, and a thrush on the window ledge was singing its beak off. Why couldn't a few rain clouds show up or the bird put a sympathetic sock in it?

Brian threw the duvet over his head. *Maybe I'll stay at home.* It would be easy to fake a cold or pneumonia or pretend his arm had fallen off. Dad was so distracted these days Brian would only have to hold it behind his back.

Except. A feather of hope tickled his chest. This was his last year at Tullybun Primary. Perhaps they'd invent a special prize for him: Quietest Pupil or Best Rescuer of Spiders from Corners. Maybe he'd win the Skinniest Legs award or, at the very least, the Most Patient Waiter for a Prize prize. Gary Budget had won the Quickest Sharpener of Pencils last year; surely the school could rustle up *something*.

He swung his legs off the bed and threw on his uniform: a white shirt, dark blue tie, grey trousers and light-blue jersey with the school motto – 'Don't You Know *That*?' – embroidered on the breast pocket. He pulled a comb through his hair, the colour of used tea bags. It flopped raggedly round his ears. Then he went downstairs to the kitchen.

What he didn't say:

'Hi, Dad. Sleep well? I didn't. I dreamed about Mum because it's the prize-giving today and I'm scared I won't win anything yet again, so it would be great if you could just pop out and buy me a cool lunch box so I can at least win *that* prize.'

What he did say:

'Hi.'

Dad looked up from … I was going to say 'his paper' or 'his coffee' because that's what most dads look up from at the breakfast table. But Bernard O'Bunion actually looked up from a slug that was gleaming on the floor like a wet wine gum. 'Hi, Brian. Sleep well?' If Dad's smile was a Maths test it would get '*2/10. Poor effort.*'

'Yep.'

Dad looked down again. He did a lot of looking down these days, and a fair amount of looking straight ahead. If Brian happened to be standing between Dad and the ahead, he told himself that Dad was looking at him. But it had been a long time since Bernard O'Bunion had looked – really looked – at his son.

'I've done your lunch.' Dad waved towards the ice-cream box on the counter.

'Thanks.' Brian knew he was doing his best. But ever since the Great Unspeakable, it had seemed as if Dad was walking through glue. Every conversation was short, every decision hard. He didn't know which potato to peel first, how often to change the sheets, whether to buy black socks or brown. Brian often ended up deciding for him, which was fine for pizza and toothpaste, but not so easy for plumbers or car insurance. And even when Dad did make an effort to do something kind, like pack his lunch, Brian usually ended up redoing it. Not right now, though. Dad would be hurt.

'What've you got today?' He really *was* trying.

'The usual,' said Brian lightly, taking a slice of bread from the counter. 'Maths. English. Geography.'

'Good,' said Dad. OK, now he'd given up – because if he'd been listening he'd know it was anything but good. The only lesson Brian enjoyed was break, when he could find a quiet spot to sit in the school garden, far from the terror of fractions and verbs and coal formation.

The garden was the school's crowning glory. As the first thing seen from the street, it was designed to create a good impression. A gardener had been hired at the beginning of the year to landscape the lawn, build a rockery and tend the flower beds. 'It only takes one small weed,' said the principal – and Brian had felt her glittering eyes on him – 'to lower the tone.'

Dad pushed his plate away. 'Have a nice day then,' he said, more to the slug than to Brian.

It had moved about a centimetre. *Poor thing*, thought Brian. *It'll take a week to get home.* He crossed the floor and crouched by the glimmering blob. Lifting it gently between forefinger and thumb, he carried it to the back door and popped it outside.

Dad stared. He bit his top lip. Then he stood up, came over and patted Brian's shoulder. 'See you later.' His voice was tight. He opened the back door and crossed the lawn to his workshop.

Idiot! Brian stuffed a fist in his mouth. *Why did I do that?* It was just what Mum would've done. She'd been a sucker for – well, suckers. And crawlers and scuttlers, hoppers and buzzers. Every tiny creature was a work of art to her, never mind if it stung or squirmed. 'Look at that rhythm,' she'd say, as an earthworm gobble-pooped soil. 'Work away,' she'd tell a mosquito that feasted on her arm. It was their complexity she loved, and their frailty. Brian could see her now, rescuing woodlice before Dad mowed the lawn or scooping up earwigs from the pavement.

An ache pressed the back of his throat. Swallowing, he opened his lunch box. Ragged ham spilled from a sandwich. There was a banana and most of a cream cracker. He trimmed the sandwich and added a biscuit. Then he

13

went into the hall, stuffed the lunch box into his rucksack and opened the door.

The air glittered as if sprinkled with sugar. A single cloud sat in the sky, lonely and sheepish as a lonely sheep. Sunlight discoed on the fence of Number Nine as Brian headed left down Hercules Drive.

Tullybun was a quiet, sensible village, the sort of place you might stop at on the way to somewhere else for a picnic of cheese sandwiches with tomato that stains the bread an alarming pink, but that you'll eat anyway because you're so bum-numbingly bored after sitting in the car all morning and there are still eighty-four kilometres to go. No film stars lived there but neither did any horse thieves. There wasn't a five-star hotel but nor was there a sewage works. While it had never won a Prettiest Village award, neither had it earned an Oh-My-Goodness-What-a-Dump-Let's-Build-a-Playground grant from the County Council.

Because it was so small – a high street with shops, a library, a church and a few roads spidering off – everyone knew where everyone else lived. Those roads were named after famous heroes, as if to make up for the village's lack of them.

The one thing the village *did* go to town on was greenery. Tullybun was bordered by fields and, at the north end, Tullybough Woods. And nearly every building, apart from the shops, had a lawn.

Brian loved lawns. They were the kind old aunts of nature: neat and calm. Reaching the library on High Kings of Ireland Street (shortened by the locals to High Street), he slipped through the gate. He stood on the grass in front of the door and took a deep breath. 'Today will be fine,' he told a blackbird. It eyed him indignantly then hopped off in a huff, as if he'd just insulted its mother (which, as it happened, he had, because 'Today will be fine' means 'Your mother is a bearded sparrow' in Blackbirdese). When Brian had said it enough times to convince himself (and offend the whole blackbird and sparrow population of Tullybun) he headed out of the gate, along High Street and into school.

Where everyone else was arriving, high-fiving, joking and joshing, pushing and squashing and ignoring Brian O'Bunion.

And where, leaning against the pebble-dash wall, he realised which prize he really deserved. *Biggest Idiot for Daring to Think That You Might Win Anything at All.*

Chapter 2

FAIL

Mrs Loretta Florris hated one thing. That may not sound like much, but believe me it covered a huge area, like a single umbrella over Ireland. Because that one thing was failure.

The principal of Tullybun Primary hated pens that failed to work. She hated ties that failed to be straight and toilets that failed to flush. Light bulbs that blew, flowers that died, rubber bands that broke: she loathed them all.

Which meant, of course, that she hated Brian O'Bunion. She hated him with an extra-special, super-size, double choc-chip hatred because he was the biggest failure in her class. You name it, he failed it: geography tests, running races, knowing when the Vikings invaded or how to spell 'exceptional'. Worst of all, he failed to pay attention.

Or that's what she thought. In fact he paid fantastic attention – just not to her. Why would he, when there were so many more interesting things to focus on?

Like the fly that was bombing the window on his left.

Compare that to the Maths sheet that lay in front of him. One was a matter of life and death, the other of mumbo and jumbo.

He looked at Question 4:

If Barry walks at 5 km an hour, how long will it take to reach his friend Zebulun's house, which is 6.34592873672984193735849287725645238373 km away? Give your answer to 14 decimal places.

Brian rubbed his forehead. *How do I know?* There wasn't enough information. What if Barry stopped at the Spar to buy a Yorkie? What if his Aunt Lettice drove past on her way to the chemist for a corn plaster and gave him a lift? What if it started to rain and he took shelter at a bus stop that turned into a flying saucer and took him to Jupiter where he spent five years digging for space turnips before returning to Earth to find that no time had passed at all? And what sort of name was Zebulun anyway?

The fly froze on the window pane. *Poor thing, it's exhausted.* Brian lifted the Maths sheet and held it horizontally against the glass. He eased the creature up and out through the little open window at the top. 'See ya.' He tickled the glass as the fly bounced away through the bright morning air.

'Brian O'Bunion.' Mrs Florris looked up from the front desk.

Twenty-four pens went still. Twenty-four heads turned. Forty-eight eyes fixed on Brian.

'May I ask *whhhat*,' the word whooshed out between tight lips, as if she was blowing dust off a teapot, 'you are doing?'

What he didn't say:

'Of course you may. And while you're at it, why not ask what my favourite pudding is, and why I hate Tuesdays, and where I keep my socks, and how many times I've seen you pick your nose when you think no one's looking? And it's very kind of you but you really don't need my permission because you're the teacher, aka God, so you can do whatever you like.'

What he did say:

'Um.'

You'd probably have said that too, for Brian's teacher was an alarming woman. I say 'woman' and I almost completely mean it because, looking at her, you couldn't help wondering if one of her ancestors had been a cauliflower. I say alarming and I *completely* completely mean it. Her hair was a helmet of solid white curls. She had a bristly chin, a thick pale neck and light green eyes like the streaky bits in marbles.

'Um,' echoed the teacher. 'Ummm. What an *interesting* word. I wonder what it means. Alec Hunratty, get the dictionary.'

Oh no. Brian lowered his head and waited for the kill.

A plump, shiny boy with a brain the size of Canada got up from his desk. He fetched the dictionary from a bookshelf at the back of the classroom.

'Please look up the word "*Um*" for us, Alec.'

He thumbed through. 'Not here, Miss.' He grinned and glowed like a toad.

'What a coincidence.' Mrs Florris licked her teeth. Chipped and yellow, they reminded Brian of cheese triangles. 'Because neither is your brain, Brian O'Bunion. People with *brains* do not wave at flies. People with *brains* do not score a year average of *twelve per cent* in Maths.'

A hiss went round, as if the room had turned into a huge slithering snake.

'How dare you downgrade my class? How dare you lower my scores with your dozy daydreaming, your dim distraction and your dense ... your dense ...' She looked round for help.

'Dullness?' suggested Alec.

'Thank you, Alec. Brian O'Brainless.' She smacked the desk. 'Get,' *smack* 'back,' *smack smack* 'to WORK!'

Brian hunched over his desk. Words and numbers danced in front of him. *I'm not going to cry. I'm not going to cry. I'm not.*

And he didn't. Eight minutes, thirty-four sniffs and not a glint of a tear later, the bell rang for lunch.

The playground was buzzing. Literally. As Brian crossed the yard he heard a low hum. It was coming from the corner where the girls were huddled round Tracy Bricket.

'Umm.' The humming got louder. 'Ummm.' Tracy's head turned. 'Oh *hi*, Brian. We were just *ummmm*ing and aahing about the prize-giving.'

Skinny Ginny Mulhinney made a sound like a balloon losing air.

Tracy smiled. 'Doesn't sound like *you'll* be winning the Maths prize.' Her eyes were so blue you could dip your toes in them.

Shoving his hands into his pockets and his chin into his neck, Brian crossed the yard. He went over the lawn to the rockery and sat down against the high-backed rock that hid him from the yard.

Worms of self-pity crawled into his mind. *Why does Florrie pick on me? Why do I care? Why can't I be tough like Kevin Catwind?* The top of his nose fizzed dangerously. He pressed his eyelids with his fingertips. *Don't even think of it*, he warned the gathering tears.

Opening his lunch box, he let out a long breath. Alone at last – or as good as. There was only the gardener pruning roses by the fence. Brian ate his banana. Checking that Mr Pottigrew's back was turned, he wrapped the skin round a garden gnome that stood by the rockery. 'Have a scarf.' There was no danger of the gardener hearing. He was stone deaf.

It had caused quite a stir when he'd started at the school. Children had crept up behind him, burping and fake farting until Gary Budget had dared Kevin Catwind to say a rude word to his face. It turned out that Mr Pottigrew could lip-read. When he'd complained to Mrs Florris, in a low drawl that sounded as if he were speaking underwater, she'd yelled at Kevin and made the whole class write out fifty times, 'I must only be rude behind people's backs.'

Brian watched the gardener bend over the bushes in search of dead flowers. He loved the clean snap of the secateurs and the way the old man laid the dead blooms in the barrow like priceless pieces of porcelain.

Mr Pottigrew straightened up and rubbed his back. He turned the barrow and wheeled it to the next flower bed. Every movement was measured and slow, as if he were rationing out his energy. He caught sight of the banana-skinned gnome, then Brian and smiled. Unlike the rest of him, his eyes were quick and bright, taking everything in, doing overtime for his useless ears.

Brian wished he could stay there all day, watching the leaves shiver under the jet as Mr Pottigrew switched on the hose and feeling the warm, furry breeze on his face. But far too soon the bell shrieked, summoning him to the awful afternoon.

Chapter 3

SUR-PRIZE

The hall smelled of wood polish and disapproval. Children thundered in and sat cross-legged on the floor below the stage. Chairs stood along the back for parents. When the pupils had calmed to a fidgeting whisper, the grown-ups filed in.

There were mums and dads. There were mums *or* dads. There were grandmas and/or grandpas. There were fifteen aunts, twelve uncles, eight-and-a-half neighbours (Mrs Mildew Pritt was very short), a reporter from the local paper and Gary Budget's rabbit called Stew who'd been smuggled in inside his mum's handbag and was now nibbling jelly beans on her lap. Anyone with any link to the school was there.

Almost.

Before you run off to ring Brian's dad and give him an earful for staying at home instead of coming to root for his child like any other decent human or pet, you'd better know that his invitation was lying in seventeen pieces in Brian's waste-paper bin. Why would he want Dad to come and watch him non-win?

Brian hugged his knees and stared at the sunbeam pouring through the window on his left. Lowering his lashes, he watched it blur to a shimmering river of dust. Imagined diving in and joining the flow, up through the window, away from the wriggling, giggling hall.

'Hey look.' There was a loud whisper – or was it a quiet shout? – from Clodna Cloot, a chunky girl built like Duplo, sitting in front of Brian. 'There's Trace's mum.'

The whole row turned round and waved. 'Hi, Sharlette.'

'You were great at six thirty-four last night.'

'I love your earrings.'

'Thanks for the sunshine.'

Tracy's mum was the closest Tullybun had to a celebrity. As the weather lady on the local news, she'd changed her name from Sharon Bricket to Sharlette Briquette and her hair from mud-brown to sun-kissed. She sat down at the back, crossed one endless leg over the other and wriggled her cherry fingernails at the girls.

Brian squeezed his knees until his arms hurt. Mum had never worn nail polish or dyed her hair. But if she'd been sitting there she'd have made Sharlette look like an old tin can.

Mrs Florris rose from the row of staff sitting on the stage. 'Attention, please.' She clapped her hands. 'Mums and dads, boys and girls, a warm welcome to our annual celebration.'

Warm? Brian shivered. Her voice was as warm as an ice cap.

'As you know, sixth class will soon be hopping from our little pond into the mighty lake of secondary school.' Mrs Florris glanced down at her notes. 'Over the last eight years, our precious little tadpoles have developed legs and arms and membranes …' a dad at the back grunted indignantly, 'er, fine brains. Their gills are glowing …' another snort, 'er, their skills are growing, and we are all very proud of our slimy young frogs.' A mum leapt to her feet. 'Er, shiny young sprogs.' Wheeling round, Mrs Florris hissed at the school secretary, 'Your typing's terrible!'

'I couldn't read your writing,' whimpered flimsy Miss Mimsy, who looked as if she might break in half.

Throwing the notes down, the principal turned back to the audience. 'The point is,' she snapped, 'we're here for prizes. Because we at Tullybun Primary believe in winning. Life is tough out there. If you don't come top, you're a flop. Who remembers the seconds and thirds, the almost-made-its, the *X-Factor* runners-up?'

'Olly Murs,' shouted Kevin Catwind.

'One Direction,' added Barry Boreen, better known as

Broadbean Barry because of his sticky-out ears.

'Silence!' Florrie glared at them, then smiled at the parents. It was hard to tell the difference. 'I am proud to have made this school a training ground for winners. And this year, as always, we have chosen those pupils who have excelled in all walks – or rather runs – of life.' She licked her teeth. 'The prize for Top Student, the person who has shown sheer, consistent, gobsmacking *clevernessss …*' she lingered on the word as if it tasted of fudge, 'goes to Alec Hunratty.'

There was faint applause. Alec won every year. Everyone knew he'd grow up to be a brain surgeon or a computer hacker. As he sauntered to the stage, Brian glanced to the back of the hall. Even Alec's parents looked bored. His mum kept typing on her phone and his dad was scribbling something – probably the square root of 7439678.2 – on the back of his hand.

'Sport.' Florrie smiled like a portcullis. 'The prize for Fastest Running, Most Goal-Scoring and Least Gasping for Breath goes to … Peter Nimby.'

'Yess!' A boy in the front row jumped up and punched the air with a skinny arm. His parents at the back did the same. In three strides Pete's long, successful legs took him onto the stage.

When the clapping had faded, Florrie grinned – or was

it grimaced? – round the hall. 'The prize for Popularity, Pleasantness and Charming the Pants off Everyone goes to Tracy Bricket.'

Tracy stood up and waved at her mum. Sharlette unleashed her super-white smile.

Everyone clapped while Mrs Florris shook the winners' hands and hung gold medals round their necks.

Then came the lesser prizes. Loads of them. By the time Florrie got to the Smallest Pupil award, Brian's palms stung from clapping. And when Clonsilla Prisk won Neatest Parting, his bottom went numb.

'Refreshments,' said Florrie at last, 'will be served in a moment.' She waved towards the tables at the side where the gardener and school cleaning lady were laying out cups and saucers.

As children turned to whisper not entirely kind things about the winners, Brian put his chin on his knees. *That's it then. Not a single prize in eight years. You'd think they could have drummed up something. Even the Best at Winning Nothing award would be better than this. If I melted into the floor right now, I wouldn't leave a stain.*

'But first,' said Florrie, 'I have one more prize to present. A new award, most dear to my heart. Brian O'Bunion, please come up.'

Brian raised his head. Had he heard right?

'Brian?' The principal frowned round the hall. Brian blinked at the window to check that another Brian O'Bunion hadn't pole-vaulted through. He stumbled to his feet.

'Watch it!' said Gary Budget, just in case Brian stepped on his foot, which he didn't. How could he when he wasn't walking but floating onto the stage?

'Ladies and gentlemen,' said Florrie, 'boys and girls. During his time at Tullybun, Brian has not found work easy.' She put her arm round him. 'But his efforts at studying have not gone unnoticed.'

Brian's chest filled up. At last: recognition that, although he hadn't succeeded, he had at least tried.

'They have, however,' the principal dropped her arm, 'gone unsuccessfully. Which is why, Brian, I'm awarding you *this*.' She whipped something out of her jacket pocket and held it horizontally between her forefingers. Bright and yellow, it was really rather beautiful, pitted with tiny holes and giving off a crisp, clean smell. 'Brian O'Bunion. It gives me *pleasure* and *satisfaction* to present you with the Lemon …' she grabbed his arm, 'for Lazy …' she opened his hand, 'Losers.' She closed his fingers round the cool, glowing fruit.

Brian had a book at home called *The Amazing Amazon*. On page seventy-three was a photo of a glass frog whose skin was completely transparent. He'd often wondered how it must feel to have your insides on show. Now he knew. Every eye in the hall could see his stomach shrinking and his guts sinking. Every ear could hear the thump of his heart and the roar of blood in his ears.

He dropped his head. A spider was edging across the stage. It raised a front leg, exploring the air. *Where's it going?* thought Brian. *What's its plan? How does the floor feel beneath its feet? Does it even* have *feet or just tiny hooks at the end of its–*

His elbow shot forward. Mrs Florris was shoving him aside. 'And now,' she told the silent hall, 'please join us for tea and cakes. Mr Ptolemy Pilps from the *Tully Tattle* is here to interview and photograph the prize-winners.' As the audience shuffled to its feet, she turned to the top trio. 'You first, dears. We'll have the faces of success on the front page.' She pinched Brian's shoulder like a crab. 'And the face of failure,' she hissed, 'on the back.'

She ushered the four children to the side tables, where Mr Pottigrew was putting cakes on a tray and the cleaner, Mrs Muttock, was pouring tea for Mr Pilps. I say pouring – more like slopping. You got the feeling Mrs Muttock didn't enjoy her job, unlike her predecessor who'd retired last summer. Miss Padder had reminded Brian of a currant bun. Soft and crumbly, with brown, merry eyes, she'd trailed the smell of melting butter through the corridors. Mrs Muttock smelled of cigarettes and disappointment, which made Brian think of her as an *un*cleaning lady.

Her eyes glittered as he approached. 'Cuppa tea – with *lemon*?' She made a rasping, gurgling sound, a mixture of cough and snigger.

Mr Pilps put a hand on his shoulder. 'Don't worry,' he murmured. The edges of his kind eyes crinkled. 'I'll take your photo to keep Mrs F. happy. But I'll make sure it doesn't go in the paper.'

Brian blinked his gratitude. He didn't trust his mouth. People were moving away from him as if he were a virus.

He waited while Alec, Tracy and Pete posed for photos, shoving their medals and grins at the camera.

Pete insisted on a picture of his bare feet. 'Unbeatable,' he bragged, waving his smelly socks in Brian's face. Smart Alec wanted a close-up of his forehead – 'so it fills the whole shot' – and Tracy's pout was like two blushing slugs.

'Now Brian,' said Mr Pilps loudly. 'Your turn.' He leaned forward and whispered, 'Then I'd get out of here if I were you.'

You bet. Parents were staring at Brian when they thought he wasn't looking and turning away when he was, their faces muddled with pity and scorn.

Florrie glanced across from her conversation with Alec's parents. 'Make sure you get the lemon in the shot,' she barked at Mr Pilps.

While the photographer focused, Brian did the opposite, letting his eyelids droop and the crowd fade to a murmuring blur that, just for a moment, numbed the needles tattooing his chest.

A tinkling crash brought him back to the hall.

'Idiot!' For once Florrie wasn't shouting at him. Mr Pottigrew was standing over a mess of smashed plates and crumbs.

The gardener had come up with a tray of refreshments for Alec, Tracy and Pete. Grabbing a scone each, they must have jostled him so that he dropped the tray. Now they stood and sniggered.

'Go and get a brush!' shrieked Florrie while the old man bent down to gather the shards and crumbs, sticky with honey. When he ignored her, she pushed through the crowd, crouched down and shoved her face into his. 'I said go … and get … a brush … you clumsy … old … *fool.*'

Even someone without any ears at all would have heard that. Blinking and nodding, he got to his feet and shuffled out of the hall.

Brian made the most of the distraction. While the principal shooed everyone away from the sticky rubble, he followed the gardener out into the corridor.

Mr Pottigrew stopped at the door of the storeroom and turned round. Brian froze. He'd held it together until now. But the kindness in the old man's eyes made his chest boil and his cheeks catch fire. He rushed on: through the entrance hall with its plaques listing past prize-winners, out the front door, across the yard and through the school gates.

He leaned against the railings. Now what? He couldn't go home, not yet. Dad would be as comforting as cardboard. 'Oh dear,' he'd probably say, glancing up from his work, or, 'Pardon?'

Brian hurled the lemon into a bush. He had to go and talk to the only three people who'd listen.

Chapter 4

CURLY WURLY SANDWICH

The first two people who'd listen lived by the church in Tullybun.

OK, maybe lived isn't quite the word. Nor perhaps is people. But listen they certainly did.

'I don't get it,' said Brian, sitting cross-legged in front of Mum's grey speckled gravestone and wrapping his arms round his knees. 'It's not like I don't try at school.'

I know, said the gravestone. Actually it said:

Lily O'Bunion, 1970-2013
Beloved Wife and Mother

But Brian knew what it meant.

He sighed. 'Is it a crime to fail?'

Course not.

'So why does Florrie hate me for it?'

The headstone thought for a minute. *Perhaps because it reflects on her. Perhaps when you fail as a pupil she thinks, deep down, she's failed as a teacher.*

Or perhaps, said the gravestone beside it, *she's just a ghastly old gherkin.* Actually it said:

Tobias O'Bunion, 1915–1994
Nimble of Hand, Simple of Heart

But Brian could read between the lines.

He reached over and patted the gravestone. 'Thanks, Grandpa.' Although they'd never met, Brian had loved his grandfather ever since hearing how he'd discovered his calling. One day at school, twelve-year-old Tobias had been chewing a piece of toffee while puzzling over a Maths problem. The toffee had fallen onto his desk. Snatching it up before the teacher could see, Tobias noticed how the sunlight danced on its delicate golden dents and twists. That was the moment he'd jumped to his feet, thrown down his pen – Brian pictured the ink freckling the floor – and marched out of school to train as a jeweller. Though he never made much money, charging a pittance for every beautifully crafted necklace and brooch, he'd loved his work and passed on his passion and business to Dad.

If only he'd passed on his courage as well. Brian imagined what Tobias would have done this afternoon. He'd never have stood obediently on stage while Florrie shamed him. No, he'd have stuck out his tongue and marched straight out of the hall.

Brian scooped a handful of soil from the grave, as if hoping a little courage might have leaked into the earth from his grandpa's bones. But it crumbled through his fingers, dry and sad and anything but encouraging.

Brushing his hands on his trousers, he stood up. They meant well, they really did, but there was only so much comfort dead relatives could bring. He blew a kiss to Mum and Grandpa. Then he walked out of the churchyard, tiptoeing politely around the other graves, and went to find the third person who'd listen, a.k.a. his best living friend.

OK, his only living friend.

Alf Sandwich worked in the supermarket on High Street. Smile-in-the-Aisle was not well named. People often went in with a grin but rarely brought one out. Instead they ran scowling down the pavement to rescue their cars before Mr Scallops, tutting and tilting his traffic warden's hat, gave them a ticket.

The cause of their annoyance was Alf. You couldn't have met a friendlier man. That was the problem. Queues would lengthen as he chatted to each customer, admiring their choice of toothpaste or advising them how to cook the parsnip they'd put on the conveyer belt. 'Wash and peel him' (vegetables were always male) 'then add a bit of oil and pop him in the oven at 200 degrees – that's Celsius of course. Cook him for, oh, I'd say fifteen minutes – no, twenty – then sprinkle on garlic and roast for another fifteen – no, twenty – until he's nice and crispy. Leave him to cool for a minute or so: don't want you burning your tongue, Mrs Dargle. Then add a bit of cayenne pepper – if you want to pop and get some now, I'll wait – and you've cooked up a feast.'

By which time he'd also cooked up a storm of furious customers. Most people avoided his till like the plague, preferring the sulky, gum-chewing services of Anemia Pickles, who looked at you as if you were stealing her oxygen but whizzed your groceries through.

Not Brian. He always chose Alf's till. He loved the old man's calm, the way he chatted and chuckled, gave you all the time in the world and didn't seem to notice, never mind care, that other customers were rolling their eyes or sighing like steam irons. If only Brian could notice or care so little at school.

'Aye Aye, Cap'n O'Bunion.' Alf raised his hand in salute as Brian joined the queue.

'Aye Aye, Cap'n Sandwich.' Brian saluted back and put a chocolate bar on the belt.

'Curly Wurly. Good choice.' Alf nodded approvingly.

'Firm and filling, light but chewy. Not like Mars bars – dense as cement. Or Toblerone – you might as well eat an Alp.'

A man in a suit coughed behind Brian.

'Curly Wurly, though, that's a winner after dinner. Nothing better with a cup of milk and honey and the nine o'clock news. I wonder if every bar's the same shape.'

Brian fingered the packet. 'I've never checked.'

The suit snorted.

Alf smiled along the queue. 'Any idea, folks?' Heads shook, toes tapped.

'For goodness sake,' muttered Snortysuit. 'I have a meeting.'

Alf didn't seem to hear. 'You OK, Cap'n?' He frowned at Brian.

'Fine.'

'Hold on. I'll be with you in a sec.'

Brian stood back while Alf served Snorty and four more customers, for once letting a melon through without remarking, 'She's lovely with a slice of ham' (fruit was always female).

When the queue was gone, Alf lifted the flap and came out from behind the till. 'Now, Cap'n, what's up?'

Leaning against the confectionery shelf, Brian told him about the prize-giving. Alf patted his arm. The back of the old man's hand was yellowish with blue veins, like those stinky cheeses that grown-ups seem to like. 'What a thing to do.' He shook his head. 'And in front of the whole school. Poor lemon too – I bet she was embarrassed.'

'No one else was,' said Brian. 'They loved it. Even Tracy Bricket, and she'd just won the Pleasantness prize – or rather the Pleasant-to-People-Worth-Impressing prize.'

'Hmm.' Alf patted his stomach thoughtfully. Round and neat, it looked as if it had been strapped on, like a giant clown's nose. 'Tracy Bricket, eh? She was in here yesterday. Her parents had a ding-dong in the household aisle. Not much pleasantness between them, I'd say. Her mum looked ready to throw the Toilet Duck.'

'At least she's *got* a mum.'

Alf opened his mouth. Then he closed it. He knew why Brian and Dad hadn't set foot in Tullybough Woods for two years, one month and nineteen days. He also knew better than to speak of the Great Unspeakable.

'Anyway.' He cleared his throat. 'Shame on that teacher of yours. What *is* she thinking of, filling your heads with all that claptrap about winning and beating each other all the time?' He shook his head. 'Imagine if I taught my girls that: Kitty or Sue, or Jenny or the twins. There'd be war.'

Alf had a huge family. That's what he called it, anyway. It lived at the end of his garden. With no children, and a wife who'd died eight years ago, the forty thousand bees in

37

a hive by the river were his nearest and dearest, the loves of his life.

'Your dad should go in and complain,' he said. 'Tell her that fighting bees make feeble honey.'

Brian grunted. 'Dad's terrified of her.' And he couldn't see Alf's bee metaphors working on the principal.

'Well he should talk to one of the governors, then. It's his duty – his *privilege* – as your dad.' Alf took another Curly Wurly from the shelf and wagged it at Brian.

'But she'll hate me even more if she finds out that Dad's complained.'

'He can do it confidentially, ask not to be named. And even if she does find out, so what? You'll be leaving the school in a few weeks.'

A tiny light rose in Brian's chest. Alf was right. Florrie had gone too far. She must be stopped, if only for the sake of future victims. *And Dad must stand up for me. That's what dads do.* 'OK.' He took a deep breath. 'I'll talk to him. Thanks, Alf.'

'Pleasure, Cap'n. Now you can do *me* a favour.' Pressing the second Curly Wurly into Brian's hand, he winked. 'Find out if they're the same shape.'

CHAPTER 5

BRAVE AS A FEATHER

The house was empty when Brian got home. Dad must still be working. Dumping his schoolbag in the kitchen, he went out the back door, crossed the lawn and knocked on the door of the workshop.

'Hi,' came Dad's voice.

Brian opened the door and breathed in the smell he'd known all his life: burnt leaves and coffee with a sour, acidic kick. He stood in the doorway inspecting the room's clutter. The drills and pliers hanging from the walls could be the torture instruments of a lunatic dentist. On his left was a machine like an old-fashioned mangle. But instead of squeezing the water from shirts and breeches, its job was to flatten gold and silver wires between the two rollers. In front of him, on a stand, was a horizontal rugby ball with ear muffs. At the press of a switch the earmuffs trembled,

39

polishing rings and bracelets within an inch of their lives. Best of all was the Table of Evil. Tucked in the far left corner, it was strictly out of bounds. Dad had warned him that the bowls of sulphuric acid and ammonia could burn your skin off. Just smelling those vicious fumes sent a delicious chill across Brian's shoulders. It was as if an invisible dragon lived in the shed.

Dad's workbench stood along the back wall. He looked round and smiled. Then he bent back over his work. Brian came over, bouncing slightly on the floorboards. Even on the grimmest days they sent little bursts of fun up your legs.

The table was a jumble of bric-a-brac: gold studs and silver hooks, screwdrivers and tubes of glue. Brian stood beside it and watched. This was where he felt closest to Dad. There was no forced chitchat, just the odd explanation here and there and a shared delight in the intricacy of the work.

'Soldering.' Dad held a broken gold ring between the finger and thumb of his left hand. With his right hand he took a brush from a pot. 'Flux,' he said, dabbing the two edges of the ring with the brush. 'It cleans the gold.' He replaced the brush and picked up a pair of tweezers. Poking them round the litter of the workbench, he found a tiny gleaming square. 'Gold solder.' He laid it across the gap in the ring. Brian watched enthralled. The steadiness of his hands, the precision of his search through the debris on the desk ... Dad truly had brains in his fingers.

He unhooked a small tube from a stand. It was wired to a foot pedal. As he pressed the pedal, a thin flame sprang from the tube. He trained it on the ring. The gas gleamed like a dragonfly's wing: blue-pink-orange. The gold square melted and sank seamlessly, filling the gap in the ring.

Dad lifted his foot. The flame vanished. 'Neat job. Mrs Griggs'll be pleased. It's her wedding ring.' He leaned back in his chair, relaxed, approachable. It was now or never.

'Dad.' Brian bit the inside of his cheek. 'Something happened at school.' Perching on the desk, he told him everything without as much as a sniff. He felt quite proud of himself.

Until he saw Dad's face. It had gone tight and small.

Brian swallowed. 'Alf says you ought to complain.'

Dad's hands, so sure a minute ago, twisted in his lap. 'Who – I mean what can I ...?'

'Tell the school governors what a bully she is. How she yells at me all the time even though I'm doing my best, I really am. It's just I'm no good at my work.'

'I know.' Dad scratched the back of one hand with the other. 'I really do.' Brian watched the skin wrinkle and redden. 'I was the same. Maths, spelling – didn't have a clue. We're not cut out for school, Brian.'

'So? That doesn't give her the right to treat me like that. Please, Dad, go in.'

'I …' Dad blinked. 'I wouldn't know what to say.'

Brian slipped off the desk. 'I just told you.'

'What if they don't believe me?'

'But it's true.' Brian glared at him. 'Don't *you* believe me?'

'Of course.' Dad's eyes were soft and scared. 'It's just I'm no good at this sort of thing.'

'Who cares? It's your job.' A bomb went off inside Brian. '*Mum* would've gone in! She'd never have let this happen in the first place. She'd have sorted Florrie out ages ago.'

Dad bunched his hands in his lap.

'But you just sit there,' Brian yelled, 'hiding behind your desk, all pathetic and hopeless and scared!'

Dad closed his eyes.

Wheeling round, Brian strode out of the workshop, slamming the door so that the whole shed shook. He marched across the lawn, numbed by the venom of his words. Then, like a wasp sting, their poison sank in. Rage and guilt fought inside him. *Dad deserved all that.* He clenched his fists. *Well maybe not all. Maybe not pathetic.* He shoved the back door open. *Or hopeless.* He ran through the kitchen and down the hall. *But definitely scared.* He climbed the stairs, two at a time.

On the landing he stopped. Instead of going into his

room and hurling himself on the bed, he crossed to Dad's – Mum's – bedroom.

Opening the door, his anger gave way to guilt. If it wasn't for him, Mum would still be here.

He sat on the bed, winded for a second by grief. Then, breathing slowly and carefully, he opened the drawer in Dad's bedside table and took out a wooden box. The lid was curved and embossed with gold like a mini pirate chest. Brian opened it. *To Lily*, it said inside, *with you know how much love. Bernard.*

Mum had once told Brian that Dad's name meant brave as a bear. 'Brave as a feather,' he muttered savagely.

Inside the box were pieces of Mum.

Before you go and ring the police, please understand that to Brian Mum's jewellery was part of her, just like her nose or her laugh. She'd worn most of it most of the time because, of course, it was made by Dad. There was the amethyst butterfly on a chain that swung forward every time she bent to kiss Brian. There were the gold bangles which clinked as she climbed the stairs, heralding the bedtime story.

But Brian was looking for something else. Closing his eyes, his fingertips explored each familiar piece. It felt as if he were touching not metal and gemstones but Mum herself. There was the sharp tip of her dragonfly brooch, and there the cold moons of her agate necklace. His fingers closed round a smooth hoop. *Yes.* He took it out, slipped it onto his middle finger and opened his eyes.

Mum's engagement ring. It was the only piece of jewellery Dad had ever bought. The oval amber, set in silver, was held by four tiny clasps. It was as plain as a barley sugar – except for one thing.

Mum had often told Brian the story of their fourth date. Dad had taken her for a picnic by the river. Kneeling down on the rug to propose, he'd been so nervous that he'd knocked over a pot of honey. She'd laughed and said, 'Oops, and yes I will.' When he'd clasped her hand and promised to make her a dream ring, she'd said, 'Thank you, Bernard, oh look there's a bee stuck in the honey.' Then she'd lifted it out and licked – yes licked – the creature clean. That afternoon, while shopping in town, she'd glanced in the window of a jeweller's shop and squealed, '*There's* my engagement ring. You don't mind, do you, Bernard? It's just so beautiful and it'll always remind me of our picnic, and you can make me lots of other jewellery, and, oh, the poor poppet, what a dreadful way to die.'

Because trapped inside the amber was a tiny honey bee.

It looked at first glance like a tangle of black cotton. But on closer inspection it took shape as a breathtaking complication of wiry legs, ghostly wings and hunched body. It was enclosed in an air bubble. Only one back leg, fatter than the others, was actually touching the amber. Mum had explained to Brian how the creature had once been caught in sticky resin, probably from a tree. The resin had hardened and fossilised around it. The jeweller had told her it was twenty million years old.

'Twenty million?' he'd gasped. 'That's older than my great-great-great-great-great-great-great-great–' and he'd gone on and on until he was gasping for breath … 'grandpa.'

The first time he remembered her taking it off was on a trip to the beach. She'd handed it to Dad for safekeeping before jumping into the sea. She might as well have pulled her finger off. Seeing Brian's shocked face, she'd laughed and said, well, yes, in a way it *was* part of her – her third most precious jewel, after him and Dad – and she'd never lose it, just like she'd never lose them.

'Except you did.' Anger boiled inside him again. He hated Dad. He hated Florrie. A tear ran down his cheek. Brushing it furiously away, he stared at the ring.

His rage cooled and hardened, gleamed and grew into a cold, smooth pearl of a plan. A plan that would stick two fingers at them both, make a fool of Florrie and make Dad super-sorry for letting him down. A plan that would bring Mum right back to his side.

Brian slipped off the ring and put it in his pocket. He closed the box, replaced it in the drawer, smoothed the duvet where he'd sat on the bed and left the room. Shutting the door softly, he crept downstairs to Dad's study. After printing what he needed from the Internet, he went back upstairs to do his homework like the good, obedient, well-behaved boy he was.

CHAPTER 6

DON'T TRY THIS ON YOUR SISTER

Dad tried to patch things up at dinner. He kept glancing at Brian with twitchy smiles. 'More potato?'

'No thanks.' Brian fixed him with cold, polite eyes.

Dad pushed a pea round his plate with a knife. On good days Brian thought of peas as little green moons, cratered and calm. But this one looked shrivelled and mean, like a mouldy belly button.

'Shall we watch *Celebrity Bathrooms*?' Dad's voice was bright and thin.

'OK.' Brian collected the plates, binned the broccoli that Dad hadn't dared make him eat and stacked the dishwasher, like the kind, helpful boy he was. He even insisted on sweeping the floor, brushing the dirt into tight piles while Dad went to the lounge and switched on the TV.

Watching Tilly Capilly pull the ruby-tipped toilet chain

47

that played her number one hit 'U Bend My Heart', Brian slipped his hand into his trouser pocket. His fingers closed round the ring.

I can't, he thought. *Dad'll be gutted. Florrie'll be livid. And Mum would be … delighted.* 'It was only gathering dust,' she'd say. Then, frowning at Dad, 'At last *someone's* standing up to that wicked old wasp.' They were the only insects she disliked. Bullybugs, she called them. 'Did you know,' she'd once told Brian, 'that bees put guards at the hive door to beat up any wasps that come looking for honey?' Then she'd shaken her head. 'It's so unfair that bees die when they sting you, while Bullybugs buzz off without a care in the world.' Brian could almost hear her adding, 'Just like certain teachers.'

When Abs Abercrunch had finished weightlifting his solid gold towel rack, Brian stood up. 'I'm going to bed.'

Dad got up too. Brian stepped back. *Don't you dare kiss the top of my head.* Dad sat down again. Rubbing his palms on his thighs, he murmured, ''Night then. Sleep well.'

But he didn't. After a few hours of restless, shimmering half-dreams in which lemon-shaped wasps chased him through a Curly Wurly maze, his alarm went off. He'd been careful to set it loudly enough to wake him, softly enough not to disturb Dad, who was the lightest sleeper.

Three o'clock. Slipping out of bed, Brian put on his dressing gown. From his desk he took the Internet instructions he'd printed out and the sponge bag he'd packed in the bathroom before going to bed. He put them in his pocket and crept through the door he'd left carefully ajar. He tiptoed downstairs and along the hall. Thank goodness the kitchen door was open; the whisper of a creak might wake Dad. Not daring to switch on the light, Brian felt his way through the darkness, his hands stretched out in front of him. At last they met the smooth edge of the fridge door. His fingertips crept round, easing it open with a sticky sigh. He held his breath. But the only sounds were the hum of the fridge and the drum of his heart. He opened the freezer section and took out the ice tray he'd filled when sweeping the floor after dinner. *Good.* The cubes had frozen. By the light of the fridge, he found the keys on the kitchen counter. He unlocked the back door, closed the fridge softly and went out.

Leaving the door open to stop the latch clicking, he stood for a moment. His lungs filled with cool, still night.

The difficult part was over. The impossible lay ahead.

When the kickboxing had stopped in his chest, he ran across the lawn, holding the ice tray in one hand and the keys in the other. Clouds stained the sky like milk on black paper. The workshop loomed from the night. Fumbling with the keys, Brian unlocked the door and climbed in. As he turned on the light, a ghostly alchemy transformed the room. Everything in it – the pine walls, the steel machines and shiny clutter on the workbench – turned to gold.

He crept across the floor. A board creaked. He froze. Why? Dad would never hear him here. It was as if the workshop itself was watching him – the tools and trinkets, bowls and machines – with glinty, probing eyes.

Brian had never been in here on his own, let alone at night. He'd always come with Dad, perching on a stool to watch him at work, heating and moulding, bending wires and twisting sheets into brooches and earrings. Dad and his tools were a magical team, conjuring beauty and order from glittering bric-a-brac. And now he was intruding on that team. He knew what to do – he'd watched Dad enough times – but would the tools cooperate with his rebellion?

Brian put the ice tray on the table. He took the ring and sponge bag from his dressing-gown pocket. Putting them on the workbench, he switched on a desk lamp and held up the ring. The amber glowed around the dark knot of the bee. From the sponge bag he removed what he'd borrowed from the bathroom: a little mirror, a bottle of surgical spirit, some balls of cotton wool and a safety pin. He stood them by the lamp.

'Stop it,' he told his shaking fingers. He held the ring between his left index finger and thumb. He slid his right thumbnail under one of the silver clasps that held the amber. 'Ow!' His nail bent uselessly. He rummaged on the desk. Finding a Stanley knife, he slid the sharp blade under the clasp. It bent back. *Yes!* He unhooked the other three. Then he slid the knife under the amber itself, easing it off the silver base. Time must have weakened the glue that held it there.

Brian sat back. *So far so good.* He held the amber up to the light, admiring the golden sheen. Inside the air bubble the bee's wings stuck out at right angles to its hunched body. Its front legs were tiny scribbles, its antennae frail threads. You couldn't have designed a more delicate jewel. Apart from that bulging back leg. It looked like the bicep of a teeny bodybuilder.

A miniature chest of drawers, like a stack of matchboxes, stood on the desk. Brian opened the drawer marked 'stems and backs' and took out a little silver circle on a stalk. Attached to the bottom of the stalk was a butterfly clasp. He held the circle against the amber. Not a perfect fit but it would do. In another drawer he found a tube of glue. He unscrewed it. His hands were steady now, intent on the task. He squeezed a bubble of glue onto the silver disc. *Perfect.* He pressed the amber against it. Glue oozed round the rim. He circled the amber with a fingertip, like a snowplough clearing a road. Then he pressed the amber to the disc until his fingertip ached. *Forty-nine, fifty, fifty-one …* when he'd reached a hundred, Brian let go. He gave the amber a little tug. It didn't budge. *Result.*

He leaned back in the chair. *Now for the fun.* He bit his thumb. *I can do this.*

Leaning forward, he unscrewed the lid of the surgical spirit bottle. The stern, cold smell was strangely reassuring. He'd like to see any germ make it past this bossy boots of a cleanser. He pressed a ball of cotton wool against the top and tipped the bottle up. Tucking his hair behind his left ear, he rubbed his lobe with the cotton wool. He took the safety pin from the desk, unhooked it and rubbed the pointed wire. He did the same for the stem of the new earring. Then he pulled off the butterfly clasp and laid them all on the spirit-soaked cotton wool. *All clean.*

The ice in the tray was beginning to melt, each cube shrinking in a rim of water. Brian popped one out easily. With his right hand he held the cube behind his left earlobe. The ice was so cold it felt hot. *Good.* Maybe this pain would drown out the next. Water dripped onto the table.

Just a quick jab. He bit his cheek. Leaning forward, he took the safety pin in his right hand, looked in the mirror and …

'Aaaaghh!' A scalding sting. The pain seemed to suck his whole body into his ear. Tears rushed to his eyes. He remembered to breathe in short gulps, trying not to move his head. Fumbling for the earring, he pushed it through the hole. Oh the throbbing weight on his lobe! He put his right elbow on the table and laid his head sideways on his palm, waiting for the pain to settle.

Surprisingly quickly it did. As he held still, it sank to an ache. He breathed more deeply. The flow of air relaxed his chest. He looked in the mirror and forced a smile. *Done it.* The earring looked as if it had always been there and the skin around it was remarkably calm, with only a slight red shine to show for the violence.

Gingerly Brian touched the back of his ear. 'Ow!' A nip of pain as the stem moved in the hole. Taking the cotton wool, he dabbed behind his ear – 'Tssss' – to clear the bits of blood and skin. Then he took the butterfly clasp and, looking in the mirror, clipped it gently and wincingly onto the back of the earring.

He soaked more cotton wool in spirit and cleaned behind his ear. Taking another clean, dry ball, he wiped the amber as vigorously as he dared. He mustn't take any chances; the smallest germ could cause infection. The amber squeaked with cleanliness. Brian rubbed again then dropped the cotton wool. There was another squeak.

He frowned.

And another. He stared in the mirror.

'YAAAAAAH!' He shot backwards in the chair.

The bee's antennae were wiggling.

CHAPTER 7

THE AWAKENING

'Well hello there.'

'Eeeeaah!' Brian's left hand flew to his cheek. *What the …?* Had the pain of piercing messed with his hearing?

'A pleasure to meet you too.'

It must have messed with his sight as well. In the mirror he saw the antennae wiggle again. He touched his earlobe. *Aaah!* Pain scorched through. His fingers were shaking too much to grasp the earring, let alone pull it out.

'Though strictly speaking, it's you meeting me. I've known about *you* for ages.'

'Uuuhhhh.' Brian's hand dropped uselessly.

'Yaaaaaaah. Eeeeaah. Uuuhhhh. You do have a way with words.' The voice was high and sharp, a needle of sound in his ear. 'Still, better than nothing after all this time.' The bee's head rose in the air bubble. Was it really, actually *talking*?

Apparently so. 'And by the way, thanks for waking me up.'

'I –' Brian swallowed. 'I didn't. I mean – did I? I mean – how?'

'With the cotton wool. Rubbing the amber makes it go all tingly.'

'It does?' Brian stared in the mirror.

'And that makes me tingle too.'

'It does?'

'Which gives me energy to talk.'

'It does?' Brian's eyes were huge and still, as if blinking might shatter the dream.

'Blessed honeysuckle!' The bee tutted tinily. 'At last someone to talk to and this is what I get. Do you think you could try a bit harder?'

Brian was struggling to think at all. Questions whizzed round his head like socks in a washing machine. 'How … who … what are you?' he managed.

'You tell me!' peeped the bee. 'Last time I looked I was a ring. Now it appears I'm a stud in your ear. What the poppy poop have you done? Your mum'll be furious.'

'No.' Despite the craziness of the conversation, Brian's breath caught in his throat. 'She won't.'

'Why ever not? You've ruined her engagement ring, for sunflower's sake!'

Quickly and haltingly he explained.

The bee was silent. Then, 'Oh. I'm sorry. Very sorry

indeed.' The squeak had softened. 'So that's why I've been in the dark all this time. I thought she was bored of wearing me.' There was a sigh. 'I'll miss sitting on that lovely finger.'

Brian swallowed. So much of Mum was fading these days. The more he tried to summon her eyes, her smile, her voice, the more they blurred into a gentle mist. Now he sensed rather than saw the slender fingers that ran through his hair as she cuddled him on the sofa. That folded his pyjamas into perfect squares and peeled neat spirals of skin from potatoes. He'd always known those fingers held magic. But he'd never guessed how much.

'Why ...' he caught his top lip in his teeth, 'why didn't Mum tell me about you?'

'Because she didn't know. I could hear *her* all the time. That's how I learned to speak. But she never quite heard me.'

'Why not?'

'Do you remember her ever polishing her ring?'

Brian frowned.

'Exactly. She hardly ever took it off – only when it might get damaged – so she never had to clean it. Soap, Fairy Liquid, they did the job for her. She only ever wiped it by chance – the odd quick brush on a towel. I hardly had the breath for a "Hi". And I was a long way off, remember, stuck on her finger not plugging her lughole. Talking of which, why *did* you turn me into an earring?'

Why indeed? Brian wound the belt of his dressing gown round his finger. He suddenly felt small and stupid. 'To get back at my dad.'

'Oh, I *seee*,' said the bee in a voice that clearly didn't. 'And how exactly does punching a hole in your ear do that?'

Brian chewed his cheek. It had made perfect sense in the heat of his rage. But now, in the cold light of almost-day, his courage leaked away. 'I guess I wasn't thinking,' he mumbled. 'I was so angry.' He told her about the prize-giving and how Dad was too chicken to go in and complain. 'Even he's scared of my teacher. She's such a bully.'

'You call that bullying?' There was a teeny snort. 'Don't make me laugh. *I'll* tell you about bull–'

But it didn't. The voice stopped.

'Hello?' Brian peered in the mirror. 'Hey!' Nothing. The bee was completely still. 'Come back!' He tapped the amber with a fingernail. 'Owww!' In his excitement he'd forgotten how sore it was. But without the distraction of a talking bug, the pain clomped back on hobnail boots. He slumped back in the chair, exhaustion flooding his mind. His brain throbbed. *I was dreaming.* He circled his forehead with his fingertips. *I must've dozed off without knowing it.*

From outside came a trickle of birdsong. A dusty grey dawn was leaking through the shed windows. Brian stood up and stretched. An ache flowed out of his shoulders.

He'd better clear up and get out of here. Dad always got up early.

Dad. Shame spilled inside him. *What have I done?* He'd be devastated by the destruction of this precious reminder of Mum. *I'll take out the earring, remake the ring.* But how? The amber was glued to its new silver setting. The day was rushing to meet him. And he was so, so … tired. A yawn tumbled out.

He stuffed the remnants of the ring and the equipment from the house into his pocket. Then he replaced the tools and left the workshop just as he'd found it, switching off the light and locking the door.

The sky was the soft grey of pigeon wings. The grass nuzzled his feet, cold and wet as a dog's nose, shocking him wide awake. *Hang on.* He stopped on the lawn. *What did the bee say? Rubbing the amber gives it energy.*

What if he hadn't been dreaming? What if the bee had just run out of steam?

The sky was lightening, unwrapping the gift of the day. A distant car sounded like tearing paper. Brian felt a glittering in his stomach, as if he'd swallowed tinsel. The air smelt sharp and promising. Anything was possible.

Even the impossible.

He ran into the house. Locking the door softly, he crept back upstairs. He sat on his bed, took the mirror from his pocket and stood it on his bedside table. He held his left earlobe gently between his trembling finger and thumb. Grabbing a corner of the duvet, he pulled it up to his ear.

And froze. There was the click of Dad's bedroom door.

'Brian?' he called from the landing. 'Was that you? I heard a noise downstairs.'

'Uh, yeah. I woke up early. I got a glass of milk.'

'Oh, OK.'

Brian waited to hear the creak of the bottom stair and the clap of Dad's slippers on the hall tiles. Then he rubbed the amber with the corner of the duvet. 'Ow! Wake up.'

Dad clattered faintly in the kitchen.

'Come on,' Brian whispered. Something wonderful had happened. Something crazy and huge that would make him special, set him apart – if only it were true. 'Please,' he rubbed again, wincing, 'you've got to.'

'I haven't *got* to do anything.'

'Yesss!' Brian felt like kissing his ear. But as that would require some tricky gymnastics, he settled for a grin in the mirror. 'I wasn't dreaming. You *are* alive!'

The bee yawned. 'I thought we'd settled that.'

'Um … not entirely.' Brian twisted the duvet in his hand. If the bee was trapped in amber twenty million years ago, as Mum had said, how could it *possibly* have survived?

The shriek, when he asked, went right through his head.

'Twenty million? You're pulling my foreleg! All I remember is that one minute I was there, alive and kicking, and the next I was here, trapped in this permanent sunset.'

'What happened?'

'Sticky situation on a tree trunk. Oh!' There was a little moan. 'If only I hadn't stopped to rest.' The bee's antennae drooped. 'I felt a trickle of goo on my leg. And next thing I knew, I was drowning. That's it, girl, I thought, you're a goner. Then everything stopped.'

'What do you mean?'

The tiny wings rose, as if in a shrug. 'Went blank. Faded out. Ended … or so I thought.'

'Until?'

'Well, according to you, twenty million years later, I was woken by an almighty jolt. The prison around me had hardened. But through it I saw something rubbing it, whizzing and pounding and polishing. I tingled all over.'

'You mean like when I rubbed your amber?'

'A thousand times harder, a thousand shocks stronger. When it stopped I saw through my golden glass that I was stuck on a silver ring. Where I've been ever since, able to see and hear but not much else without an extra rub.'

Brian frowned. How could making the ring have brought her back to life?

'Twenty million years, eh?' The pointy head lifted towards

the mirror. 'Looking good, if I do say so myself. Except for that leg.' Brian guessed she meant the fat back limb. 'But what's a girl to do, glued in gum with no chance of a workout to empty her pollen sac?'

He grinned at the thought of a bee doing leg lifts.

'It's no joke,' she snapped. 'Do you know the last thing Nora said to me? "Stick around, Pie Thigh."'

Brian turned his giggle into a cough.

'Our Nora had more sting in her tongue than her tail. Same with my other sisters, all thirty-five thousand, four hundred and twenty-six of them. And Mama Humsa was the worst of the lot.' The bee sniffed. 'Never knew my dad. I must get my gentle ways from him.'

Gentle wasn't the first word that sprang to mind. But Brian managed not to say so.

'Sweet in nature, sweet in name,' she piped. 'Which, by the way, is Dulcie.'

'Dulcie.' Brian liked the way it rolled round his mouth. 'Hi, Dulcie. I'm Brian.'

'I know that!' squeaked the bee. 'And your dad's Bernard, and you have no sisters or brothers, and there are seven pebbles on your bathroom shelf that you collected from the beach when you were five, and your mum sometimes mistakes – *used* to mistake – the white one for soap, and you prefer crunchy peanut butter to smooth, and your

61

mum dries – *dried* – cups by stuffing the whole tea towel inside and twisting it round.'

Brian bit his lip. He'd forgotten how Mum did that.

'Not bad, eh?' Dulcie clapped her antennae. '*And* I was only half-awake. Amazing what you notice with a nimble mind like mine.' She sighed. 'The only nimble part of me since I was trapped in this–'

'Shhh!' Brian clapped a hand to his ear. There were footsteps on the landing and a knock at the door. *Oh no.* What was Dad doing? He never came up here in the mornings. Brian slipped into bed, raking hair forward over his ear. Thank goodness Dad kept forgetting to take him to the barber. 'Yeah?' He pulled the duvet up to his chin.

The door opened. Dad came in with a tray. On it was a glass of orange juice and a plate of toast. 'I made you breakfast in bed.'

Brian frowned. When had Dad last made him breakfast, let alone in bed? *Of course. This is a sorry for not going into school to complain. Pathetic.*

But useful too. It saved him eating with Dad and risking the discovery of his earring, at least for now. 'Thanks,' he said, taking the tray. 'Oh, and Dad?'

'Yes?' He turned eagerly in the doorway, as if hoping for a word or look of forgiveness.

'Can I borrow your phone? I need to check something for homework.'

'Of course.' Dad brought it over with a sheepish smile. He'd been promising to buy Brian a mobile for the last three months but hadn't quite got round to it.

'Thanks.'

When Dad had gone and the door was closed, Brian went on to Google.

'What are you doing?' peeped Dulcie.

'Wait.' Slowly and carefully he typed:

What happens when you rub amber?

He scrolled through the results. Next to the heading **HowStuffWorks**, a word caught his eye:

Electricity

Ignoring Dulcie's 'What?' and 'I never learned to read, you know,' he went onto the site. There were lots of complicated words like 'Van de Graaff generator', 'protons' and 'triboelectric'. But halfway down the screen, a sentence jumped out.

If you rub a piece of amber with soft cloth, the amber will develop a static charge.

Brian wasn't sure what 'static' meant, but he knew that 'charge' had something to do with electricity. Could the buffing and buffeting by the polishing machine when she was made into a ring have electrified her teeny heart into beating again?

'Wow,' she squeaked when he told her his hunch. 'Clever thinking. I like your style, Brian O'Bunion. I could get used to living with you.'

Clever? He couldn't remember the last time that word had come his way. His own heart raced. Never mind Dad, never mind Florrie. He could face anything with this tiny, tetchy miracle in his ear. Excitement sat like an egg in his stomach, smooth and glowing and ready to crack.

CHAPTER 8

VICTORY

'What. On earth. Is *that*?' Florrie's face was a Kit Kat length away. 'I can't. Believe. My *eyes*.' They were gleaming like glaciers. 'You will. Remove it. *Immediately*.'

What Brian didn't say:

'Yes, of course, Mrs Florris. What was I thinking? I'm so very sorry. I'll take it out at once.'

What (very quietly) he did say:

'Only if the girls remove theirs.'

Florrie gasped. The class gasped. The cactus on the front desk gasped.

'I *beg* your pardon?' Florrie's knuckles went white, pressing into Brian's desk.

'I said.' He blew upwards, sending his fringe flying. 'Only if–'

'I HEARD YOU!'

And then he was squashing against the back of his chair, blinking at her reddening face and wondering how her mouth could move so fast while her eyes stayed so still, and noticing that each hair on her chin wore a little trembling jacket of powder, and finding that by staring at those jackets he could ignore the words that were spilling from her mouth like pins from a box, and imagining what Dulcie, uncharged but conscious in his ear, must be making of all this hullabaloo.

Florrie paused for breath.

'He's right.' Broadbean Barry, whose dad was a lawyer, didn't even put up his hand. 'If the girls are allowed to wear them, so's he. Otherwise it's discrimination.'

There were murmurs. Most of the girls had pierced ears.

When wise people like you, and occasionally me, are annoyed by something that's not dangerous or cruel or in need of a good scratch, they do the wise thing and ignore it. But despite her sensible heels and the rain hat she carried whatever the forecast, Mrs Florris was not a wise person. She stood by Brian's desk and shrieked about the nerve, the mouth, the cheek, the lip, until she'd almost described a whole face. Then she moved down the body to screech about the kick in the pants of decency, the shot in the foot of order and the slippery slope from earring today to hooligan tomorrow to prison next Thursday blahdy-blahdy-blah.

At last she ran out of words.

Now what? Broadbean was right. And everyone knew it.

There was nothing she could do except stand there, stiff and silent with rage.

After eight seconds she sniffed. After twelve she wiggled her shoulders. After twenty-three she wheeled round and strode to the front.

She sat behind her desk. 'Homework.' She spread her palms on top. 'Geography.' She licked her teeth. 'On page forty-eight of *Don't You Know Where That Is?* you'll find a map of Europe. For every country I want you to learn,' she took a deep breath, 'the mountains the lakes the inlets the outlets the imports the exports the main sports the highways the holidays the rainfall the snowfall the crops the shops and the,' she smiled, 'favourite. Types. Of cheese. Got that?'

Only Alec nodded. He alone had written it all down.

'Because if you haven't, too bad.' Her eyes were ice pops. 'There will be a test tomorrow. And your mark will go on your final report.'

Brian's heart punched like a fist. *Victory!* His plan had worked: the girls-wear-earrings argument had stumped her. She was powerless, helpless, piling on homework because that was all she could do. His report would be rubbish anyway. He had nowhere to fall. A chain snapped inside him – of fear and control. He was free to soar into the limitless sky of rebellion, to fly where he liked, do what he wanted – eat chips off page forty-eight, or fold it into a paper crab, or use it as loo roll. He didn't care how she punished him. He'd beaten her in front of the class and that was all that mattered. He knew it, she knew it and so did they.

In the silence of Maths, he drew Florrie's face as a pie chart and cut her into twenty-five slices, one for each pupil. Reading *Peter Pan* in English, he made her walk the plank and jump to the mercy of twenty-four crocodiles. And in history he could almost hear the classroom court crying, 'Bravo!' as he sentenced Witch Florribus to fifty years tied to the back end of a cow.

So when Clodna Cloot said, 'Well done, Braino,' on the way out to break, it took him a moment to work out that she didn't mean it. And when Broadbean added, 'Yeah, thanks for ruining my TV tonight,' Brian thought for a second that he was truly grateful.

But when a football slammed into his back and Kevin Catwind yelled, 'That's for the map, Brainless,' Brian began to suspect that the class wasn't wholly on his side. And when Skinny Ginny shouted across the playground, 'How d'you spell nightmare? B–r–i–a–n,' he finally understood that he had twenty-four fewer school friends than the none he'd had before. Or, to put it more positively, twenty-four devoted enemies. Dodging the tennis ball that was rushing to greet his shoulder, he ran across the yard to the lawn. He sat down behind the rockery.

Twenty-four enemies. And one new friend.

Grabbing the edge of his sleeve, Brian brought it to his ear and rubbed the amber. The sting-ache made him hiss. He rubbed again.

'Of all the –!' A voice exploded minutely in his ear. 'How dare she speak to you like that!'

'I told you she hates me,' said Brian with a grim kind of triumph.

'What about me?' piped Dulcie. 'A kick in the pants of decency, am I? A shooter in order's foot? A hooligan-maker, a prison-pusher? Why the dandelion didn't you charge me up? I'd have given her a taste of my tongue. She's an insult to bee-manity … to humanity … to me-and-you-manity! Ooh, if only my butt was free, I'd sting her where the sun don't shine.'

Brian couldn't help smiling. He didn't doubt it for a minute.

'Oh no.' His smile vanished. Three figures had appeared on the left. He hunched against the rockery wall as Alec, Tracy and Pete crossed the lawn in front of him. He could do without more sarcastic comments.

He needn't have worried. They didn't notice him as they headed towards the row of cypresses that marked the end of the school grounds.

The trees were where you went to share gossip or

homework: a dark, private borderland, officially out of bounds. But if you managed to creep in without being spotted by the teacher on yard duty, you were safe. On the far side of the trees a narrow path ran along the school fence. Anything messy or broken was dumped there, out of Florrie's failure-hating sight: the school dustbins, the gardener's tumbledown shed, old benches and broken desks. Brian had only once plucked up the courage to creep through. He'd stood on the path and gazed into Finn McCool Lane, where graffiti and dog poop reminded him that there was life outside school, even at one o'clock on a Wednesday.

Brian watched the trio disappear into the trees. Pete and Tracy must be going to copy down the geography homework from Alec, and probably pay him for the favour. Teachers' pets couldn't afford bad marks.

'They've gone,' he whispered, dropping his hand from his ear.

'You know, you've got more guts than the rest of that class put together,' Dulcie squeaked.

'I have?' Apart from the ones that sometimes twisted inside him, he wasn't aware of any.

'And brains.'

'Really?' He'd often doubted he had any of those at all.

'Making a fool of her without breaking the rules. "Only

if the girls do" – brilliant!' Dulcie cleared her tiny throat. 'I must say, it's an honour to be your earring.'

Brian tried to smile. But he was so unaccustomed to compliments, it got tangled up and came out as a kind of wriggle across his face. 'Thanks. And it's an honour to be your ear, I mean your home, I mean–'

'What you mean, young bud, is my friend.'

Brian nodded so hard his wriggle untangled. 'Yes.' He grinned. 'I do.'

'You do what?'

Brian jumped up. He hadn't noticed Mrs Muttock creeping across the lawn from the trees. Smoking was banned in school, of course. But Brian had often seen the cleaning lady sneaking off with a hand in her pocket or caught the bitter whiff as she slunk down the corridor.

Now she smiled. 'Talking to yerself, eh? First sign of madness.' She gave a wet cackle. 'Still, I s'pose there's no choice, if no one else will.' The cackle turned into a rattling cough. Pressing a fist to her mouth, she slithered away.

Brian cupped a hand to his ear. 'You couldn't be more wrong,' he thought, 'you slimy old stink bomb.'

CHAPTER 9

GETTING AN EARFUL

The next two days were brilliant, or as brilliant as anything at school could be, which on a scale of one to dazzling was somewhere around dim. But that was good enough for Brian because Florrie didn't know what to do with him. She was stumped. So, in a surprisingly wise move for someone without any wisdom, she left him alone.

Which meant he could sit at the back of the class and cheer silently as his favourite ant outran its neighbour down the leg of his desk. He could wink at the notches in the floorboards, imagining they were the eyes of a pine monster that one day would rise up and swallow the teacher. When she came in wearing a bright red jacket, he pictured her as a strawberry flan and drowned her in a mind-jug of custard.

By the third day he felt so invisible that he was tempted to recharge Dulcie for a chat during class. But he stopped himself. Her voice may be tiny but it was piercing too. What if it reached the huge ears of Broadbean at the desk on his left? Or Kevin in front, who was training for the All-Ireland Nose-Picking Championship? And even if it didn't, what was the point? Brian could hardly chat back. It might expose her or, at the very least, prove to the class that he was bonkers as well as brainless. And that was the last thing he needed, because now they hated him more than ever.

It wasn't just because of the Geography test, in which even Alec's top score was only 54 out of 200. Now that Florrie was ignoring him, her cruelty was finding new targets, some of them surprising.

'Tracy Bricket, take those fingers out of your mouth!'

Everyone looked up. The winner of the Popularity, Pleasantness and Charming the Pants off Everyone prize was always biting her nails, but Florrie had never told her off before. Tracy's hands dropped to her lap.

Two minutes later they were back at her mouth.

'I said *stop* it!'

The PPACTPOE prize-winner was staring out the window. Mrs Florris marched over. Her neck shot forward like a desk lamp.

'What?' Tracy's eyes were as round as paddling pools. 'Oh. Sorry.' Then she did the worst thing possible. She yawned.

To Mrs Florris, a yawn wasn't just a stretch of the mouth. It wasn't an extra gulp of oxygen or a friendly sort of moo. It was a failure. A failure to listen, a failure to hear. A failure to grovel, a failure to fear. A failure to worship, respect or revere.

'Tracy Bricket, I will *not* be yawned at. Go and stand in the corridor.'

The only sound was the screech of Tracy's chair pushing backwards. Brian smiled as she passed his desk, forgetting all her unkindness in a rush of sympathy. *Boy, do I know how you feel*, said the smile. But her eyes were fixed on the door.

He tried again at break. Finding her alone, for once, at the edge of the playground, he summoned his courage and said, 'Don't worry. Florrie'll get over it.'

She glared at him. 'Bog off.' Tucking a silky strand of hair behind her ear she marched away.

Anger blazed through Brian. *Bog off yourself. I was only trying to help.*

The anger flickered and died. What did he expect? He should've known his pity would be as welcome as a wart. In its place rose triumph, creamy and sharp like sour milk. *Now you know how it feels*, he thought as she joined Skinny Ginny and Clodna who were whispering together on the lawn.

He had the same feeling next morning when Florrie handed back their essays on 'The Sweetness of Neatness'. Brian's page, normally a bloody battlefield of corrections, had no red marks at all, as if she hadn't even bothered to look at it.

She prowled up to Smart Alec's desk. 'Disappointing,' she slammed his book down, 'is *not* the word. Especially in light of the title. Smudges everywhere, and pages two and three were stuck together. No, Alec, the word is *dismayed*. What *were* you thinking of?'

There was a long silence while Alec stared straight ahead. It was strange. For once the boy who knew most of the words in the dictionary seemed unable to find a single one.

For the rest of the day, while she barked and bellowed at everyone else, Brian had a busy and fruitful time. By three o'clock he'd:

1) drawn a picture on his desk of a charging beast with white bubbly hair and labelled it 'The Florribull';
2) noticed clouds in the shape of a poodle, South America and Broadbean's right ear;
3) helped two spiders out the window;
4) watched Mr Pottigrew mow the lawn, make three trips into the trees to empty the wheelbarrow, pat the rockery gnome twice and scratch his beard four times.

Walking home, Brian realised it had been his best day for ages. Not a single telling off. And so what if no one had talked to him since Tracy? It was better than being insulted. A smile spread inside. The sun on his face, the tickling breeze, the thrill of his new secret: rebellion had brought nothing but good. It had silenced his enemies and woken a friend. He couldn't wait to charge her for a chat in the safety of his bedroom.

He unlocked the front door.

'That you, Brian?' Dad called from the kitchen.

Duh. Who else has a key? 'Yep.'

'Want some tea? I'm just boiling the kettle.'

'No thanks.'

'How was your day?' Since when had Dad cared? All this sudden effort – the timing couldn't be worse. Sighing, Brian dragged himself to the kitchen. Better stick his head in and say hello to ward off more visits to his bedroom.

Dad's smile was carefully bright. 'School OK?' The kettle shuddered to a boil.

'Yep.'

'Got much homework?'

'A bit.'

'Sure you don't want tea?' Dad lifted the kettle.

'No, I'm fine.' Brian raked his fingers impatiently through his hair. 'I'm just going up to my … *Dad!*' Boiling water was pouring onto the floor.

Staring at Brian, Dad righted the kettle and replaced it on the counter.

Oh no. Brian clutched his ear. He'd been so careful to cover it until now.

'Her ring.' Dad's face was all trembly, like its reflection in a pool.

Brian turned and fled upstairs. Sitting on the floor of his bedroom with his back against the bed, he grabbed the mirror from his bedside table. Then he pulled the corner of his duvet and rubbed his ear.

'Well, what did you expect?' squeaked Dulcie. 'Cheering and clapping? Dancing in the dahlias?'

'Thanks,' Brian snapped. 'That really helps.' He rubbed his temples furiously.

'Look,' she peeped more gently. 'He's bound to be upset. He'll get over it. And it serves him right for not standing up for you.'

'You think so?' Brian looked in the mirror.

'Of course.' Dulcie tutted. 'Shame on him. But I'm glad he didn't go in and complain. If he had, you'd never have met me.'

Brian couldn't help but smile. He knew that this was the proud little bug's way of saying *she* was glad she'd met *him.*

'Now.' She wiggled a front leg. 'Buzz off downstairs. You two need to talk. This is the perfect time.'

She was right. The earring could lead to only one subject. Brian stood up slowly. He straightened the duvet, replaced the mirror on the bedside table and walked to the door. It was time to speak about the Great Unspeakable.

Dad was sitting at the kitchen table, staring into his cup.

'I'm sorry,' said Brian, standing in the doorway. 'I was just really mad.'

Dad put up his hand as if stopping traffic. 'We'll say no more.'

'Please, Dad. We need to talk about–'

Dad smacked the table. 'It's done, Brian. You can't undo it.' From the look in his eyes, Brian knew he didn't mean the earring. Dad could easily turn that back into a ring. Mum's death crashed over him again. *It was my fault. That's what he's saying.* Brian felt as if he couldn't breathe, trapped under a familiar tower block of guilt over what had happened. He found his usual escape route: anger. 'Fine.' He spun round. Dad didn't want to talk, so they wouldn't – ever again.

At least, not properly. The odd word was unavoidable. But apart from that, Brian did pretty well over the weekend. Their longest conversation was:

'Chips or spaghetti for dinner?' (Dad.)

'Don't mind.' (Brian.)

'Are you sure?'

'Yep.'

'OK.'

Thank goodness for Dulcie. In between bossing and fussing, she proved to be a surprisingly good listener. Over the next two days Brian found himself talking about his dreadful mixture of guilt over Mum's death and anger at Dad for not forgiving him. He told her all sorts of things about Mum that he'd never dared bring up with Dad. And as he did, fading memories returned. Mum pinning flowers to her hat so that butterflies would come to feed. Mum making a ladybird climbing-frame from toothpicks. Playing Frisbee with a pizza. Wearing bubble beards when she did the washing up.

By Sunday evening Brian felt better than he had for months. Talking about Mum had melted the edge of his pain. And now that he'd stood up to Florrie, there was no one to fear.

Walking into school on Monday, he found himself whistling. Sitting at his desk, he found himself sucking a peppermint. Watching Florrie peck to the front like a constipated hen, he found himself sniggering. All of which were normally unimaginable offences.

But today, it turned out, wasn't normal.

The teacher reached her desk and turned round. 'Did anyone see Alec over the weekend?' Heads shook, brows wrinkled.

'Why?' asked Kevin.

'Because,' she said slowly, placing her palms on the desk, 'his parents just phoned. They haven't seen him since Saturday.'

CHAPTER 10

HEARTENING HONEYCAKE

It was a higgledy-piggledy, itchy-twitchy, restless mess of a day. The sort of day that, if it was human, would be sent out of class for flicking paperclips round the classroom.

While the children whispered and fidgeted, Mrs Florris shouted more than ever. She shouted at Clodna Cloot for writing too slowly and at Gary Budget for writing too quickly. She shouted at Skinny Ginny for sneezing, at Kevin for sniffing and at a stapler for running out. She shouted at the moss that had died on the nature table at the back of the classroom. And she shouted at Tracy for gazing out the window. 'You do not come to school to gaze, young lady. Gazing is not an exam subject. Gazing does not improve your grades.'

'What?' Tracy gazed at her.

'Pay *attention*!' Mrs Florris's fingers closed round a rubber. Her fist rose.

Like a many-limbed creature with a single lung, the class held its breath. She wasn't actually going to …?

There was a knock at the door. The teacher's hand dropped. Garda Poggarty came in.

You may not have heard of Tullybun's annual Favourite Grandpa competition. And if you say you have, then you're lying, because there wasn't one. What was the point? Filo Poggarty would have won every year. A round, smiley man, he looked more like an overgrown robin than a garda. His grey hair stuck out in feathery tufts. His jacket was always open, flanking his stomach like too-small wings. His cheeks were two little sunsets.

He was the best and worst policeman you could imagine. Best at helping old ladies across the road and cats down from trees. Worst at catching vandals and robbers who had plenty of time to run away, and even stop to buy a Twix, as he shuffled after them. No one could be scared of Garda Poggarty.

Except Brian O'Bunion.

It wasn't the hair or the smile, the stomach or the cheeks. It was the job. Brian had been terrified of the gardaí ever since the Great Unspeakable. Of course Dad hadn't reported the truth about Mum's death. But Brian knew the police would discover it one day. They had to. It was only fair. And then he'd get what he deserved.

But he wasn't going to help them find out. And until that day, he'd vowed to lie low. He slumped in his chair as Garda Poggarty shuffled to the front of the class.

'Sorry to bother you, Mrs F.' He wasn't smiling today. 'Just a quick word.' His eyebrows were little nests of worry.

'Of course, Sergeant Poggarty.' Florrie had put four tablespoons of sugar in her voice.

He looked gravely round the room. 'As you probably know, one of your classmates has been, er, temporarily mislaid. I'm here to ask if anyone might know anything at all about his, ah, movements since Saturday.'

Heads shook. Bottoms squifted (shifted squirmily) and shirmed (squirmed shiftily) in seats. Clodna fiddled with her pencil case as if, perhaps, Alec was hiding inside. When no one spoke, Garda Poggarty took a notebook from his jacket pocket and wrote for what seemed like a month.

Oh dear. Brian swallowed down the guilt he always felt when something went missing in class. *Was it me? Have I forgotten that I kidnapped Alec by mistake on Sunday?* As far as he could remember he'd spent the morning in Smile-in-the-Aisle, showing Alf his bee earring. (Uncharged. Brian couldn't trust even his best two-legged friend with his best six-legged one.)

At last the garda closed his notebook. 'Thanks for your time, folks. And don't worry.' He glanced at Florrie. 'There's bound to be a simple explanation. Alec probably went to stay with an aunt or a friend and – ahem – forgot to tell his parents.' The sergeant didn't look as if he'd fooled even himself. 'I'm sure he'll turn up very soon. Eh, Mrs Florris?' She nodded in a noble, law-abiding way.

But he didn't. And for the rest of the morning it wasn't only Brian who failed to concentrate. The class was one big fidget, twiddling its twenty-five pens and biting its fifty lips.

When Florrie ran out of shout, she ordered them outside. 'Four times round the yard.' She was a great believer in physical pain to restore peace and order.

But it did just the opposite. Peace and order would mean Unbeatable Pete coming first, like he always did in anything involving legs. Today he came fourth. When Mrs Florris yelled at him to pull his socks up – not easy, considering they were ankle-length – he looked at her in bewilderment. Then he bent forward, as if to do that very thing. But instead of reaching for his ankles, he sat cross-legged on the ground and rubbed his eyes.

'Get up at once!' screeched the teacher. 'Resting is not on the school curriculum. I will *not* have resting in my class.'

At the end of school there were twice as many parents as usual at the gates. Word must have spread about Alec's disappearance. Not as far as Number Six Hercules Drive, though; Dad was nowhere to be seen. Slinging his schoolbag over his shoulder, Brian hurried along the pavement, his nerves nibbling his insides. What if Alec's kidnapper was here on High Street, lying in wait for another victim? What if he or she was disguised – as that sweet little lady going into the post office, for instance? She might *look* like Miss Emer Pipette, retired teacher and the secretary of Tullybun's Small Fruits Appreciation Society, but perhaps beneath the strawberry headscarf and kindly smile lurked a ruthless child trafficker. Perhaps the real Miss Pipette had been kidnapped too.

Hang on. Brian stopped. Who said Alec had been kidnapped? Maybe he'd run away from home and left a note.

Dear Mum and Dad,

You guys are boring. School's boring. This whole lousy village is boring. I'm off to seek my brainy fortune.

Your loving son, Al.

No. If that was the case, Sergeant Poggarty wouldn't have suggested Alec might have gone visiting and forgotten to tell his parents. It sounded as if the gardaí were clueless. But a person couldn't just disappear like that, without *someone* seeing or hearing something, could they?

Who better to ask than the man who watched Tullybun

come and go? Brian hurried along High Street to Smile-in-the-Aisle.

'Aye Aye, Cap'n.' Alf waved from the till.

Mrs Clattery scowled as he dropped her packet of All-Bran to stand and salute. Brian saluted back.

'With you in a sec, Cap'n.' Alf sat down again and scanned the packet. 'Bit clogged up are you, Mrs C? All-Bran's your man. You'll be running like the Liffey in no time.'

When she'd marched out, red as a pepper, Alf popped a 'Till Closed' sign across the conveyor belt and came out. 'Heard about Alec? Dreadful business.'

'What do you know, Alf?'

'No more than you, I dare say. His mum was here this morning asking if I'd seen him in the shop over the weekend. She said he didn't come down to breakfast Sunday morning. She thought he was having a lie-in. When he didn't appear at lunch, she thought maybe he'd gone out early to meet one of his friends. It wasn't until the afternoon that she phoned him. But he hadn't taken his mobile.' Alf shook his head. 'I mean what kind of parenting is that? They've only got three kids. Talk about hands off.'

It wasn't like Alf to criticise, but Brian knew how much he disapproved of the Hunrattys' relaxed attitude. If he could, Alf would buy a cell phone for each of his forty thousand bees so they could keep in touch while foraging for nectar. It was true that Alec's parents hadn't seemed very interested at the prize-giving. Brian recalled his mum fiddling with her phone and Mr Hunratty writing on his hand. But even if they didn't show it, they must have felt proud of their son. *Unlike Dad*, he thought. *Would he even notice if I went missing? And there's only one of me.*

'You OK, Cap'n?' Alf patted his shoulder. 'Look, I'm just finishing my shift. Why don't you come round for a cuppa? Looks like you could do with a slice of Dr Alf's Heartening Honeycake.'

Brian nodded. 'I'd better tell Dad.' *As if he'll care.* 'Could I borrow your phone?'

While Alf handed over to Anemia Pickles, Brian called home.

Dad answered after ten rings. 'No problem. See you later. Bye.'

Alf lived in a ramshackle cottage at the edge of the village near Tullybough Woods. With their soft glades and secret light, the ancient woods had once been Brian's favourite picnic spot. Not any more. After the Great Unspeakable he'd never set foot in them again.

They had tea in the back garden. The air was squeaky with sunlight. Rose bushes spilled shadows onto the sloping lawn. At the bottom the River Tully ran past, dark and gleaming like a film reel.

Alf cut a slice of cake and pushed the plate across the table.

'Thanks.' Brian lifted the golden wedge.

'Watch out!' Alf's hand shot forward. He flicked at a bee that was nibbling the icing. 'Buzz off, Sue.'

'Aah!' Brian dropped the cake. The bee ambled off through the air. 'I nearly swallowed her.'

'Ugh.' Alf's smile vanished. 'My poor Susie.'

Brian had been more worried about his throat. But he knew better than to say so. 'How on earth do you know that was Susie?'

Alf cut another slice of cake and put it on a plate in the middle of the table. Four bees settled on top.

'There you go, girls, feast your feelers on that.' Alf pointed to them in turn. 'Claire, Edna, Jan and Beyoncé. *Course* I know my bees. And I'd know if one went missing too.' He gazed at Edna – or was it Beyoncé? – as she probed the dips and mounds of the cake with her antennae. 'That's the saddest part. Alec's parents not noticing for nearly a day.' He rolled a cake crumb between his finger and thumb. 'They're worried enough now, though. Poor Mrs Hunratty. She was wrung out this morning. Can't have slept a wink. She kept saying, "You're sure, Mr Sandwich? You're sure you didn't see him?" Like if she asked enough times, she'd get the answer she wanted.'

On Brian's list of top ten favourite people, Alec came fifty-third. But he had to agree it was a terrible thing. 'I wish I could help,' he murmured.

'Me too, Cap'n.' The old man sighed. 'But what can we do except keep a look-out and pray he comes back soon?'

CHAPTER 11

RESINATING

'Little madams! Who do they think they are?'

Sitting on his bed after dinner, Brian was beginning to wish he hadn't woken Dulcie. He'd looked forward to hearing her views on the disturbing events. He knew she'd have plenty. Her crankiness was strangely relaxing – with enough huff for both of them, she saved him the effort – and it was comforting having someone there who'd shared every part of his day. But he hadn't bargained for this.

'Pampered brats. Fancy the old duffer knowing all their names!'

'He may be old but he's not a duffer!' Brian glared in the mirror on his wall. 'He's the kindest man ever.'

'I can see that. Their own slice of cake indeed – their own plate! In my day we had to work for our food. No wonder those girls are so hefty.'

Brian hadn't noticed any flab on Alf's bees. But it wasn't the moment to mention it.

'And that apartment block!' He guessed she meant the hive by the river. 'Ready-built walls and roof – I ask you. Probably furnished too.'

Brian swallowed a smile, picturing TVs and sofas in each tiny cell.

'No such mollycoddling in my day. We had to build our own home, every cell and comb. We bees are supposed to work for a living – we're *called* workers, for daisy's sake! But that lot are more like shirkers. No distant foraging for them, oh no, but flowers sitting pretty on their doorstep. Ooh!' Her wings fluttered. 'If I could get out, I'd teach 'em a thing or two, show 'em how to bee.' She shook her head furiously. 'Bet they can't even dance.'

'Dance?' Brian hooted. 'Why would they?'

Dulcie stamped her front legs so hard that his earlobe wobbled. 'You mean you've never heard of the waggle dance?'

Brian shook his head and sucked in his cheeks, picturing Dulcie in a tutu.

'I thought life was supposed to have evolved since my day,' muttered the bee. 'More like *diss*olved.' She tutted. 'A bee is born to dance. She needs nectar and pollen for food, right?'

Brian nodded.

'So she flies around looking. And where does she find them?'

'In flowers.'

'Very *good*.' Dulcie clapped her antennae sarcastically. 'When a bee finds a crop of flowers she buzzes back to the hive and dances up and down the honeycomb. And the way her bottom waggles tells her sisters where to go.'

'Are you serious?' Brian's eyes filled his face. 'That's incredible.'

'But true.' She sniffed proudly. 'Our butts are moving maps. At least ...' a tiny sigh tickled his ear, 'they're meant to be. Mine never was.'

'Why not?'

Her wings drooped. 'I was the youngest and smallest, the runt of the family. And that's saying something, out of thirty-five thousand, four hundred and twenty-six.'

Brian murmured sympathetically. He felt runty enough in a family of two.

'From the moment I popped from my cell, my sisters bossed me around. They gave me the grottiest jobs: waxing the walls, polishing their wings, emptying our ... you-know, from the comb.' Brian tried to picture bee poop. Chubby nuggets or skinny threads?

'Meanwhile my sisters crept and crawled to our queen-mother. They were desperate to win Mama Humsa's favour. I didn't get a look-in.'

Brian felt a pang for this teeny Cinderella.

'But she didn't care about any of her daughters. Her only interests were eating and sleeping and being adored. Whoever brought the most nectar was the favourite. One day it was Melanie, the next Fran, the next Arabella, that silly, frilly furball.' Dulcie squeaked contemptuously. 'And because I was too young to fly, I was bottom of the heap, bullied like you wouldn't believe. "I've got wing itch," they'd say, "scratch it, Dulce." Or, "My cell needs rewaxing. Get to it, maggot." And when they weren't bossing, they made fun of me. "Found any nectar, wimpywings?" or "Hey, sucker, you wouldn't know a pansy if it punched you in the mandible."'

Brian winced. Thirty-five thousand, four hundred and twenty-six classmates.

'It was a hot, dry summer. The flowers were few, the pickings low. And the hungrier we got, the more I was bossed. It became unbearable. I started to wonder why I'd bothered being born. I mean, what was the *point*?'

Brian stared in the mirror. 'You too?' It may have been twenty million years ago, and it may have been only a bee, but boy was it comforting to know that another living thing in the history of the universe had wondered the same thing.

'I couldn't wait to fly,' said Dulcie. 'To whizz off and escape their bullying. I tried every day but my wings were too weak. Until one morning ... aaahh.' A ripple ran through her antennae. 'My whole body rose and my legs left the ground. I'll never forget that first flight.'

Brian closed his eyes. Lifting his arms, he flew with Dulcie. A paper-dry breeze blew through his mind. He danced on a cushion of air.

'I'd never felt so free,' she said. 'I decided I wouldn't go back. I'd buzz off and join a new colony, a crowd that would treat me well, never mind that we weren't related.'

'Good for you.' Brian thought of Dad. Family could be overrated.

'So I chose a route to avoid my sisters. Whenever I saw one I veered off. They'd only fault my flying, say my wings were too slow or my bottom too low. I worked with the breeze, letting it lead me far away. Until suddenly I caught a smell. A whiff of sweetness on the air.'

Brian sniffed. But the only whiff he caught was of dirty socks scattered over the floor.

'I followed the scent to a glorious sight. Candles of white on a carpet of green. Don't ask how but I knew, I just knew, it was clover. I dived in and gorged. I stuffed my mouth with nectar and my sacs with pollen.'

Brian tasted the sweetness on his tongue, felt the weight on his legs.

'And when I'd finished,' Dulcie peeped, 'I knew what I had to do. Fly home and dance, lead my sisters to food.'

Brian's eyes sprang open. 'What? I thought you wanted to find a new family.'

She sighed. 'Family. That was just it. I suddenly knew that I couldn't let them starve. Mean as they were, they were all I had.' She shook her head. 'Oh, I can't explain. It was a buzzing in my blood, a stirring in my heart that I had to help my own kin. And something else too.' She fixed him in the mirror with her gleaming eye. 'This was my moment, my chance to shine. To strut my butt and prove my worth.' Her voice was getting softer. 'To be the bee I was born to be. That I never,' she gasped, 'got … to be.'

Brian looked in the mirror. She'd gone silent and still. What a moment to run out. He grabbed a corner of the duvet and rubbed the earring.

'I flew back as fast as I could,' she squeaked on seamlessly. 'As the nest came into view, I stopped on a tree trunk to catch my breath. Disaster. That's when the goo trickled onto my leg.'

Brian frowned. 'Couldn't you just pull it out?'

'You think I didn't try?' snapped Dulcie. 'Look at it, puffy and packed with pollen. That's when Cleo flew past. I shouted for help. But she just laughed and carried on.'

Brian imagined Dulcie wriggling and shrieking after her sister.

'Then the twins came by. I was up to my chest now, but

together they could've pulled me out. I begged and promised to show them a feast. But did they believe me? Did they Sweet William!' She snorted. 'Laura and Nora just sneered and jeered, rolled their eyes and slapped their thighs.'

'Bees have thighs?'

'This isn't easy.' Dulcie gave a little sob. 'Allow a girl some poetry. I begged and wailed but on they sailed. Another blob fell, and another, covering my mouth, my eyes, my feelers. I thrashed with all my strength and managed to clear a small airspace round my body. But it was no good. I was caught forever, stuck in muck with no chance to dance.'

Brian saw her head droop in the mirror. *Poor thing.* What a terrible memory to haunt her forever, trapped in this eternal prison. If only he could say or do something to help.

He smacked the duvet. *Of course!*

If he was officially brainy, you'd say it was a brainwave. But as he officially wasn't, let's call it a Brianwave. 'Why didn't I think of it before? I'll crack the amber and let you out.'

'NO!' The shriek was a skewer through his head.

When the ringing had stopped, he said, 'Why not? You could dance your butt off.'

'I wouldn't *have* a butt! Or a head or a thorax. After all these years, I'd probably just crumble to dust. The amber's the only thing holding me together.'

'Oh.' The Brianwave crashed and died. 'I hadn't thought of that.' His shoulders slumped. 'I was only trying to help.'

'You can. Help me look for Alec.'

'What?' Brian blinked in the mirror.

'It strikes me we could both do with a mission, something to make us feel useful. And what could be better than this?'

Brian stared at her. She was right. Imagine the praise, the fame, the acclaim, if they were the ones to find Alec. 'But how? No one seems to know anything. Where would we start?'

She waved a front leg airily. 'We'll work out the details later. Just picture the headline: "Boy Makes Beeline for Missing Mate".'

He did. And it sure looked good, not to mention un-characteristically modest, coming from this proud little bee. 'Or "Bee Makes Boyline",' he said graciously.

'No way!' she squealed. 'I'm not being splashed across the papers, thank you. Who knows who might steal me for scientific research? I'll lie low in your ear and direct you from here.'

'Direct me where? If Alec's parents and the gardaí don't know where to look, how will we?'

Dulcie yawned. 'Let's sleep on it. I'm sure we'll come up with a plan.'

You'd better, thought Brian, reaching for his pyjamas. Because when it came to detecting, he didn't have a clue.

Chapter 12

NOT A TRACE

Luckily Dulcie had enough ideas for both of them next morning. When Brian rubbed her awake on the pillow she was buzzing in her air bubble, thrilled to get her mandibles into a project.

'We need to put out feelers,' she said as he threw on his uniform.

'I haven't got any,' he reminded her, buttoning up his shirt.

She tutted. 'How *do* you manage? Well then, I guess your eyes will have to do.' Grudgingly she added, 'I've noticed you don't use yours too badly.'

Brian blushed. It may not sound much of a compliment, but for someone who got an average of minus four a month, it was praise indeed.

Luckily too, Dulcie's mind was methodical. 'Remember I spent my early days cleaning and tidying. Organisation is the key. We need an HQ for Operation Find-Alec.'

Brian loved the idea of turning his bedroom into a

command centre. He was Sherlock, he was Poirot, he was Double-O-Bunion. Pulling his tie rakishly to one side, he scanned the room. *It needs to look more professional.* He should lose that *Star Wars* cushion for starters, buy a finger-print kit and replace the *Doctor Who* poster with a map to stick pins in, like they did in war films.

But Dulcie would have none of it. 'Use that brain of yours,' she squeaked. 'The first rule is secrecy. What if your dad comes in? We don't want him nicking our clues, telling the gardaí so they can steal our glory.'

Brian blinked in the mirror. 'You really think we can beat the police?'

'Course we can – because we've got a great big ace up our sleeve. School.'

Brian could think of several words to describe school, but ace wasn't one of them. 'What do you mean?'

'Well, where does Alec spend most of his time?'

'Home. And school, I suppose.'

'Exactly. We can't go snooping round his house. But imagine if someone at school knows something … something they want to hide. You're the perfect spy. Lurking in corridors, listening in the yard – easy as pie because, no offence, everyone ignores you.'

A sour-sweet smile rose in Brian. Being invisible had its uses.

With secrecy paramount, the command centre was downgraded from the bedroom to the back of the *Doctor Who* poster. And by the time Brian shoved it under the bed it was even less impressive.

Questions	Answers
1. When did Alec disappear?	Between Saturday night and Sunday afternoon
2. Where?	Dunno
3. Why?	No idea
4. How?	Haven't a clue
5. Who could be involved?	Anyone
6. Suspicious-looking characters	Everyone

'It's a start,' said Dulcie as they headed downstairs to breakfast. 'Now keep your eyes skinned and your ears pinned back. Who knows what we'll find at school?'

Nothing, it turned out, except long faces and short fuses. The children huddled in jittery groups, speculating wildly.

'Maybe Alec ran away.'

'To join the circus.'

'Maybe his nan took him to Barbados and forgot to say.'

'Maybe he went to Hollywood,' said Skinny Ginny, who dreamed of going herself, 'to audition for the *Muppet Hunger Games*.'

'Quiet!' Florrie flew in. Her normally rock-hard hair stuck out in wispy tufts. 'Not a peep from anyone today. Thanks to your parents I haven't slept a wink.' She clutched an imaginary phone to her ear. 'What are you doing to protect my Barry, Mrs Florris?' Broadbean blushed. 'How do I know my Clodna's safe?' Clodna's eyelids fluttered clumsily, like swing-bin lids in a breeze. 'As I *gently* reminded them,' the teacher snapped, 'Alec went missing from home, not school.' She glowered from the front desk. 'I am *fully* confident he'll be back before home time. And you are all *perfectly* safe.'

Oh dear, Mrs Florris. Fail. And fail again. Because Alec was still missing when the last bell rang. And the next day there wasn't a Trace.

Everyone thought she was off sick. She'd been out of sorts for a few days, with all that yawning and gazing. And in the Land of Florrible, unwell was short for unwelcome because illness, of course, was another kind of failure. 'Studies show that the common cold can lower your Maths score by twelve per cent,' the teacher told them at least once a week. 'A verruca can spoil your spelling – how *do* you spell verruca, Barry? … There is no record of Albert Einstein ever having piles.'

So it wasn't until ten past twelve, when her mum stuck her head round the door, that anyone thought twice about Tracy.

'Sorry to disturb,' said Sharlette Briquette. She came in holding a pink lunch box. 'Tracy forgot her–'

'Tracy?' Mrs Florris's eyebrows collided. 'She isn't in today.'

Sharlette blinked slowly round the class. Her lashes could have swept the floor. 'What do you mean? She left as usual this morning.'

'What I mean,' said the principal in a flat grey voice, 'is that she isn't. In. Today.'

'Are you sure?' Sharlette's voice was bright red.

'Mrs Briquette. Your job is to know where the rain clouds are heading. *My* job is to know who's in my class. And I can assure you that your daughter is not. Nor has she been all morning.'

Sharlette ran a hand through hair the colour of Crunchie filling. 'So where is she?'

Not in the corridor. Not in the hall. Not in the staff room or the secretary's office. The cloakrooms were empty and the other classrooms full – of children who weren't Tracy.

When Florrie went out with Sharlette to phone the police, the class sat strangely still and silent.

The principal came back alone. 'The gardaí have advised us to close the school today.' For once her voice was soft. 'The secretary is texting all parents to collect you at lunch time. Those of you with mobiles, please call them now. Those of you without can use the office phone.'

It was the 'Please' that did it. Florrie never said please.

Nobody spoke. But everyone knew. There were two missing children now.

Brian joined the queue for the office phone. When he rang home there was no answer. He left a message on the answerphone.

'No one's to leave until their mother or father arrives,' said Mrs Florris as the bell rang for lunch.

It was chaos at the gate: parents jostling, children shoving, hands held and hugs hugged. But there was no sign of Bernard O'Bunion. Despite the teachers' efforts to fasten every child to its parent, Brian managed to slip through the crowd and out the gate.

Trust Dad. He stomped along the pavement. *The only no-show.* He dodged a car door that swung open across his path.

'Watch it!' yelled Mrs Budget, a small but mighty woman, bundling Gary into the back seat. Scowling at Brian, she slammed the door.

'Thanks for the lift,' muttered Brian. *How dare Dad not come!* He kicked a pebble into the road. *He got the text like everyone else.* He strode down High Street, past the library – even the lawn looked anxious today – past the bank and the shoe shop, too furious to worry about being kidnapped by any pedestrians disguised as old ladies or pigeons.

Reaching Smile-in-the-Aisle, he stopped. *Why should I go home?* Why not let Dad wonder, just for a bit, where he was, and whether he could have disappeared too? *Serve him right.* With a rush of hot triumph, Brian marched into the supermarket.

But Alf wasn't there: not at the till annoying customers, nor stacking shelves or sweeping the floor.

'Called in sick,' snapped Anemia Pickles from her till. 'I mean, fanks a mil.' She chewed her gum like a lion chews a zebra. 'I'm on me own 'ere.'

Brian nodded and turned. *Perfect.* He'd spend a few hours at Alf's house and, oh dear, forget to tell Dad. That would give him a kick in the parentings.

CHAPTER 13

NIBBLES AND TROUBLES

Brian knocked three times on Alf's door, shiny and red except for pale streaks where the paint had scabbed off. No answer. He knocked again. At the ninth knock, when he was just deciding that the human race had its limits, there was the sound of slow footsteps. The door opened a crack. A white face peered round. White as paper. White as snow. White as flour – because that's what it was. Alf's face and hands were covered.

'Aye Aye, Cap'n'. His salute sent a cloud into the air.

'Are you baking?' said Brian. 'Anemia told me you were sick.'

Alf smiled sadly. Little cracks appeared in his white lips. 'Baking, yes. Sick … in a way.' His mouth twisted oddly. 'Don't want you catching it. See you soon, Cap'n.' He pushed the door.

'No!' Brian stuck his foot in the way. 'Please let me in.'

'I can't.' An astonishing tear snaked down Alf's white cheek.

'Why not?' Brian pushed his foot against the door.

Alf looked up and down the street. Flour sailed off his forehead. 'Just for a minute then.'

Mystified, Brian followed him down the narrow hall to the kitchen.

Alf had indeed been baking. There was flour on the table, the chairs and the floor. The kettle and stove had a sprinkling. A sweet cushiony smell filled the air.

'Hang on.' Wiping his cheek with a sleeve, Alf took a tea towel and crouched by the oven. He opened the door and brought out a tray of scones, lumpy and golden like rocky suns. 'Nothing beats a nibble when you're in a bit of trouble.' He slid a knife under each scone and lifted them, one by one, onto a cooling rack on the counter.

Brian sat at the table. 'What trouble?' He'd never seen Alf sad, let alone tearful.

The old man brought out two plates and knives, a saucer with butter and a pot of honey. He sat down heavily opposite Brian. 'Sergeant Poggarty came round. Said he had a few questions. Said ...' he picked up a knife and put it down again, 'I was seen chatting to Tracy in the shop. And Alec too, last week. And that someone heard me inviting you over. That it was just a formality but–'

'But because you're kind to children you must be a kid-napper!'

'No no. Well, not in so many words.' A tear plopped onto the table.

'Outrageous!' Brian smacked his hand down. A knife bounced in alarm. 'How *dare* anyone suspect you! I'll go and tell them you'd never, ever–'

'No.' Alf raised a hand. 'As I say, it was a formality. I'm sure the gardaí are talking to everyone. Just a bit upsetting, that's all. But nothing compared to what Tracy and Alec's families must be going through.' He shook his head. 'Lord help 'em.' Pushing his chair back, he stood up and shuffled over to the counter. He put the scones on a plate and brought it to the table. 'There you go, Cap'n.'

Brian sliced his scone and plastered each half with butter. He spread honey on top and took an angry bite.

Alf was right: a nibble was good for trouble. The fluffy warmth soothed his indignation. Sergeant Poggarty was only doing his job. But Alf of all people! He was part of the furniture, safe as the sofa in Tullybun library. The gardaí must be desperate. Two disappearances and no one seemed to have a clue.

Except. Brian took another bite. Could two disappearances be a clue in itself?

Alf buttered his scone slowly, covering every golden

ridge and dip. 'No one's ever vanished from the village as far as I can remember. And that's pretty far.'

Brian finished his scone. *Tracy and Alec. Why them? It's not as if they're friends.* He licked the last honey off his knife.

Alf smiled. 'I feel better for talking. Thanks for your kindness, Cap'n.' Bits of scone were stuck between his teeth. He loosened them with his tongue. 'They should teach it in school. More use than long division.'

Brian snorted, imagining Florrie. 'Did you just share your Lion Bar, Brian? A+ for being a pet.'

Pet? Brian's fingers tightened round the knife. *That's it.* Alec and Tracy may not be friends, but they did have something – or rather someone – in common.

Surely not. A terrible thought danced through his mind. So terribly terrible – and deliciously delicious – that he couldn't possibly share it with another being until he was sure. Not a human one, at least. He fingered his earring. 'I'd better get going,' he said. 'Dad'll be wondering where I am.' *As if.* 'Thanks for the scone.'

At the front door Alf scanned the street. 'Don't tell anyone you came round. It wouldn't look good right now.' He patted Brian's shoulder. 'Glad you did, though. As they say, a snack shared is a problem halved.'

Brian had never heard that one. And far from halving, the problem had multiplied into something far more thrilling.

He walked down the road. After a few paces he turned to check that Alf had closed the door. Then he rubbed his ear with his sleeve. 'It's obvious!' he hissed.

'What is?'

But before Brian could explain, Mrs Alveola Fripp turned into the street. The founder of the 'Tullybun Says No to Gum' campaign was on her daily round, unsticking grey blobs from fences and pavements and fixing them to her forehead, in order to remind villagers that 'Chewing gum is the acne on the face of the earth'. Catching sight of Brian, she nodded in greeting. A blob dropped from her brow. As she bent down to retrieve it, he hurried past.

Arriving home breathlessly, he unlocked the front door and went upstairs.

'Brian?' Dad called from the kitchen. 'Did school finish early?'

Brian stopped on the landing. 'You didn't get my message then.'

'No. What happened?' Dad came to the bottom of the stairs. 'How awful,' he said when Brian told him about Tracy. 'Two children missing.' He put a hand to his cheek. 'What's going on?' He began to climb the stairs. 'Brian, be careful. I can't bear to think of–'

'There was a text too.' Brian's voice was icy. 'You were supposed to collect me from school.'

'I was?' Dad stopped on the third stair. 'I – I'm sorry.' He laid his hand on the banister. 'I was in the workshop. I left my phone in the house.' His eyes were bright with a focus they'd lacked for months, as if he'd woken from a long sleep.

Brian held his gaze. This was the bit where Dad would say, 'I forgive you for what happened, Brian. Let's move on.' You could almost hear the violins.

A funny little muscle moved in Dad's cheek. 'You're not to walk anywhere alone. I'll drive you to school.' The light went off in his eyes. He turned down the stairs.

Brian marched into his bedroom and slammed the door. 'Why can't he *talk* to me?' he said, rubbing his earring roughly.

'You weren't exactly Mr Let's-Be-Friends,' said Dulcie. 'And stop rubbing so hard. You're giving me the jitters. Now tell me what's so obvious.'

Brian's anger gave way to excitement. He kneeled by the bed and pulled out the *Doctor Who* poster. 'Mrs Florris,' he said, pointing to questions 5 and 6 on the list.

'That hideous old hornet – what about her?'

'She's the link between Alec and Tracy. I mean, they're both teacher's pets.'

Dulcie's wings fluttered irritably. 'You're saying she likes them so much she kidnapped them? Funny way to show you care.'

Brian frowned. He hadn't thought of that. He'd so wanted Florrie to be the villain, he hadn't been thinking straight. His shoulders sank. The excitement leaked out of him.

Almost. Something still glimmered inside, the ember of a thought that refused to die, that smouldered and glowed and sprang into flame.

'Oh!' He clapped a hand to his mouth. 'You don't think–'

'I certainly do. All the time. Not much else to do in here.'

'No, I mean, you don't think that …' Brian jumped up. 'Come on!' With shaking hands he pulled off his shoes, praying that Dad had gone back to the workshop. He mustn't hear a thing; he wouldn't let Brian out alone now, and there was no time to explain.

He crept downstairs, carrying his shoes, and out the front door. Slipping them back on, he ran down Hercules Drive.

'Blinking buddleia,' gasped Dulcie as he panted out his fear. 'I see what you mean. Quick!'

He was. But it still took ten minutes to get to Hannibal Crescent. He turned into Caesar Close.

He stopped dead. *I'm too late.* His insides collapsed like wet sand.

A garda car was parked by the kerb outside Number Twelve. Two neighbours stood on the pavement. Their

111

arms and faces were folded tight. Brian recognised old Mr McDooly, the greengrocer, and tiny Mrs Mallows.

Drooly McDooly waved across at Brian. 'Hey, lad, what are you doing here?' His bald head glowed like an onion in the evening light. 'You shouldn't be out alone.' Brian didn't move.

'Another one gone,' said Fontania Mallows. The president of the Tullybun Nitting Circle, a group of retired women who met every Tuesday to teach head lice to circle dance, pressed her hands to her cheeks.

Brian stopped himself from blurting out, 'I know.' Instead he managed, 'When?'

'Lunch time. His mum was waiting at the gate but he never came. The principal rang the guards.'

That rules Florrie out, thought Brian. *Why would you abduct a pupil then phone the police?*

'How do you know all this, Fontania?' Mr McDooly looked impressed.

'I was, er, watering the roses. I heard Sandra Nimby over the wall. One tries not to listen but –' she tutted sympathetically, 'she was slightly hysterical.'

How can you be slightly *hysterical?* wondered Brian grimly.

Not that it mattered. The point was that if he'd been smarter, thought faster, had a bigger brain, he could have stopped the disappearance of Unbeatable Pete.

'Hold on, lad.' Drooly shuffled into the road. 'I'll walk you back.'

But Brian was already legging it miserably home.

CHAPTER 14

EARSHOT

If you're hoping for a quiet night of misery, there's nothing worse than a bee buzzing encouragement in your ear. Especially one that recharges every time you turn your head on the pillow. After an hour of tossing and turning, all Brian's efforts to look on the downside had been ruined.

'OK, we got there too late,' Dulcie chirped, 'but at least it backs up your hunch about teacher's pets. That's the only thing that links Alec and Tracy and Pete.'

'We don't know that,' said Brian. 'What if they meet outside school? What if they all go to dance classes, or Scouts on Fridays, or Tiddlywinks Club?' Rolling grumpily onto his back, however, he couldn't quite picture Alec doing Zumba or Tracy sleeping under canvas or Pete winking tiddles. Surely three such different people were unlikely to hang out together. *Which is good news and bad*, he thought, staring into the darkness. Good because it meant that school was the best place to start looking. Bad because no way would it open tomorrow. After all, what sort of principal would put her precious pupils at risk?

Hmm, that's a hard one. Let's see now …

'Closure,' barked Florrie on the local radio news next morning, 'spells failure.'

'Really?' Dad's coffee cup paused at his mouth. 'I thought they began with different letters.' Was that a bad joke or bad spelling? You couldn't tell with Dad.

'At an emergency staff meeting yesterday,' the teacher's voice continued, 'we at Tullybun Primary resolved not to be defeated.'

You mean you *resolved.* Brian nibbled his toast. *And everyone else was defeated.*

'Let me assure parents,' Brian pictured her tongue licking her teeth, 'that school is the safest place to be. Pupils must be delivered to and from the gates, where there will be a heavy police presence.'

The heavy police presence was high-fiving children as Dad dropped Brian at school. Ignoring Sergeant Poggarty's smile, Brian hurried through the gates. He bowed his head to hide the blush that would announce his crime, the greatest ever committed – and yet to be discovered – in Tullybun. Perhaps the judge would shave a few years off his sentence if he found the missing children.

But how? Crossing the yard into school, Brian discovered

how hard it is to find a clue when you haven't a clue what *is* a clue. Could it be that furry tennis ball stuck behind a drainpipe? Or the apple core rusting in the corner of the cloakroom? How about the drawing pin upturned on the corridor floor?

By lunch time he'd narrowed it down to three:

1) the spot on Clodna Cloot's chin – it definitely wasn't there yesterday;

2) the Dairy Milk wrapper under Kevin's desk – ditto;

3) Gary's new elephant pencil sharpener that pooped shavings when you twisted the trunk.

Which all added up to … Brian chewed his pen and did some complicated Maths … three red herrings. Sighing, he took out his lunch box and went to the yard. Children were crowding round Sergeant Poggarty, trying on his hat and blowing his whistle. Brian slipped past them and ran across the lawn to his favourite spot. Sitting with his back to the rockery, he took out a sandwich.

A fly landed on the crust. It jerked across the bread like a badly made cartoon. Brian waited for it to stuff its tiny face then brushed it gently away. 'My turn.' He bit into rubbery cheese. Then he pulled down his left sleeve and rubbed the earring. 'Nothing,' he sighed. 'We're getting nowhere.' He took another bite and gazed ahead at the row of cypresses. They rose in a dark green screen, protectors of privacy and goodness knows what secrets.

Hang on. He stopped chewing. *That's where they went in the other day, before they all disappeared. And where –* he swallowed – *Mrs Muttock came out.* She hated children. She didn't seem too keen on grown-ups either, or smiling or jokes or sunny days or Fridays, or any day, come to think of it. A chill fizzed across his shoulders. Could she have done something to them in there?

'I don't see how,' said Dulcie when he shared his suspicion. 'She came out just after they went in, remember? And from the other side. They were on the left; she came out on the right. She didn't have time to do anything.'

Relief and disappointment swilled through Brian. Dulcie was probably right.

Probably. A string vest of a word: not tight-fitting like definitely, but full of holes and dangling threads. *Probably* left room for doubt. And besides, whatever Mrs Muttock did or didn't do in the trees, she was still the sneakiest snooper in school. She reeked of sneak, she stank of snoop, as she crept round eavesdropping on private conversations and oozing out of corners when you least expected her. She was certainly worth investigating.

Five minutes later he was in front of the cleaner's

storeroom. He knocked softly on the door. No answer. He glanced up and down the corridor. Then he turned the handle.

It was more of a cupboard than a room. Sweet and harsh smells crashed up his nostrils: lemon floor polish and bleach, pine air freshener and cigarette smoke. The shelves on his left were stacked with bottles and sprays of Dettol, Windolene and Mr Sheen. Mops and brushes leaned against the right-hand wall. In front of him was a chest of drawers. Brian opened the top drawer. Inside was a packet of cigarettes and an ashtray. In the next drawer lay a pair of rubber gloves and–

'Oy!' Fingernails bit into the top of his arm. 'Get outta there! Whaddyou think you're doin'? I'm reportin' you to the principal.'

Brian slammed the drawer on his finger. 'Ow!' The pain made him brave. 'And I'm reporting *you* for smoking in school.'

'Shh!' She shut the storeroom door. 'Keep it down. I'll lose me job if she finds out. Now you better tell me what the blinkers you're up to.'

Brian backed against the chest of drawers. She was far too close. Her nose was a river delta of veins.

'What were *you* up to?' The words fell out of him. 'The other day. In the trees.'

'Eh?' She scratched her cheek. 'What are you on about?'

There was no going back now. 'You came out when they went in. And now they've disappeared. If you don't tell me, I'll go to Sergeant Pogga– arrghh.' He shrank against the chest of drawers as Mrs Muttock raised her arm. Cramped as it was, there was room for a strangling.

''Ow dare you suggest …?' Her arm dropped. 'What d'you *think* I was doin'? 'Avin' a fag, of course. Needed some privacy with 'er Majesty on the prowl.'

Is she telling the truth? The disgust that twisted her face at the mention of Florrie suggested she was. 'What did you see?' said Brian.

'Just the three of 'em wanderin' into the trees.'

'Did you tell the police?'

'Eh? Why would I? Friends are always sneakin' in there together.'

'But that's the point.' Brian pressed his hands against the chest. 'They're not friends.'

''Ow'm I supposed to know that? I'm your cleaner not your classmate. And they were thick as thieves at the prize-givin' last week. Smarmin' up to 'er Majesty. Laughin' at poor Mr P. when 'e dropped the tray.'

Brian remembered the gardener hurrying out of the hall, oblivious to their taunts but all too aware of Florrie's fury. He recalled the old man's look in the entrance hall suggesting that, although he couldn't hear, he could see more than most.

Brian stood up straight. *Perhaps he did.* The gardening shed was behind the trees after all.

He glanced at his watch. Ten minutes until the end of break. If he could get out of here, he might have time to find Mr Pottigrew and ask him, slowly and face to face, whether he'd seen Alec, Tracy and Pete in the trees and what they'd been up to.

'I'd better go,' he said awkwardly. As he slid past, she gripped his shoulder. 'Not a word about me smokin', not a word about your snoopin'. Deal?'

'Deal,' he gasped, holding his breath to block out the bitter smell.

Mr Pottigrew wasn't in the front yard or the back. He wasn't watering the grass or weeding the rockery. Brian looked across the lawn. Perhaps he was in his shed, safe from the slave-driving eyes of the principal who disapproved of any form of laziness such as having lunch or sitting.

Brian glanced back at the yard. Checking that no one was looking – they were all too busy playing Frisbee with Sergeant Poggarty's hat – he ran towards the cypress trees. He slipped into a sharp, sweet darkness of silky prickles and soft earth. The sounds of the yard faded. Coming out the other side, it felt as if school had slipped off him like a loud, garish cloak.

The path ran from left to right in front of the wrought-iron fence. Brian flicked a twig from his hair and looked to the right. Flies scribbled above a huddle of dustbins. Beyond them stood the shed. Mr Pottigrew was sitting on a deckchair in front. His head rested against the back and his eyes were closed. Little snores bubbled from his lips.

Brian walked towards him. He didn't like to wake him, but this was important.

As he passed the dustbins the bell rang. *Stuff it. I'll just have to be late for–*

He froze. Then he dived behind the dustbins. He crouched between two green bins, trying to make sense of what he'd just seen.

Mr Pottigrew's head jerking up at the sound of the bell.

Was that a coincidence?

There was one way to find out. As the gardener rose from his chair, Brian spread his palm on the gravelly ground. His fingers closed round a handful of stones. *Don't make a noise.* He peeked round the bin. A stale stink filled his nose – of who-knows-what mouldy lunches, gone-off milk, dried-up glue and other school debris.

Mr Pottigrew had gone into the shed. He must be putting the deckchair inside. Brian's heart hoofed it round his chest. He'd always been the world's worst shot. Now he had to be the best. Lifting his arm, he flung the stones towards the shed.

There was a machine-gun rattle. *Shot!* They'd hit the corrugated iron roof. Brian hunched more tightly.

Mr Pottigrew came out of the shed. He frowned up at the roof then looked both ways along the path.

Silence roared in Brian's head. *Don't move. Don't breathe. Don't exist.*

He managed the first two as Mr Pottigrew took a bunch of keys from his pocket and locked the shed. Then the old man turned left along the path, away from Brian – *thank goodness* – and past a gate in the fence.

Brian darted across the path and into the trees, praying that the not-so-deaf gardener wouldn't hear the thundering of his heart.

CHAPTER 15

WOOD YOU?

Brian didn't have a clue what lesson it was, or what home-work Florrie had just written on the board, or how many months there were until Christmas.

But he did have a clue. The question was what to do with it.

As he sat at the back of the class, through whatever subject it was that involved a large amount of shouting, a medium amount of tooth-licking and a small amount of jabbing Gary's arm with a ruler, three options came to mind:

A) ignore it: forget that he'd just seen a deaf man hear;

B) tell Sergeant Poggarty;

C) confront the gardener himself.

He frowned. A) was impossible. How could he forget what he'd seen? B) was pointless. The police had already questioned all the staff. So either there was some perfectly reasonable explanation that Brian couldn't think of right now, or Mr Pottigrew was hiding something – in which case he'd lie again, both to the police and to Brian – which meant that C) was a waste of time too.

Staring out the window, he came up with D). More snooping.

When the last bell rang, Brian grabbed his school bag, ran to the cloakroom and stuffed it into his locker. Then, instead of joining the froth of children pouring into the front yard, he slipped down the corridor and out the back door. He ran across the empty yard, over the lawn and into the trees. On the far side he crouched in the gloom and looked along the path.

Sweat tickled his palms. It was what he'd hoped and dreaded. Mr Pottigrew was there, locking up the shed with a key from a bunch. He turned left down the path and stopped at the back gate. With another key he undid the padlock.

Brian's heart didn't know whether to leap or dive. So it settled for both, bouncing like a basketball in his chest, kicking up a dust of indecision. *Now what?*

Dad would be waiting at the front gate. Brian should turn round, tell the gardaí what he'd seen, go home and live happily ever after.

Except that he wouldn't – because ever after would be anything *but* happy unless he did something about it.

He fingered his ear. Dulcie would know what to do.

His hand dropped. There was no time to talk. Mr Pottigrew had locked the back gate and disappeared from view. And besides, it was clear what to do.

He crept across the path, crouched by the dustbins and looked through the fence. Mr Pottigrew was getting into a small grey car.

No! It hadn't occurred to him that the gardener might drive.

As the car drove off slowly down Finn McCool Lane, Brian climbed onto one of the dustbins. Wedging a foot between two rungs, he hauled himself over the fence. He dropped to the ground and crouched behind a bush by the railings. Maths may be a disaster and spelling a no-no, but climbing he could do.

Too well. Mum's face drifted across his mind.

When the car had turned left into High Street Brian darted down the lane and stopped at the end. The traffic was bad; he could follow the car easily, melting into the crowd as it stopped for red traffic lights and pedestrians who spilled dozily across the road.

At the top of High Street it turned right into Gandhi Way. Brian walked faster. With fewer shops and pedestrians here, the car went faster and it was harder to hide. He kept his hands in his pockets in what he hoped was a casual way, and his eyes on the car in what definitely wasn't.

Mr Pottigrew turned left into Joan of Arc Avenue where the shops gave way to houses. Brian followed in a kind of creeping trot that must look very odd. The car disappeared right into Spartacus Lane, where the houses gave way to bushes. *No, I'm losing him.* Brian broke into a run. He couldn't keep this up for much longer.

He didn't have to. Entering the lane, he saw the car turn left and disappear down a narrow track. The engine stopped. He heard a door open and shut. A lock clicked faintly. Then silence.

Brian counted to five. Then he scuttled along the pavement to the entrance of the lane.

Thank goodness there was plenty of cover. The hedgerows spilled ivy and sweet smells onto the path. Brian hid behind a clump of ferns. The little car was parked behind a tree at the side. Mr Pottigrew was about ten metres ahead, approaching a gate into a field. At the far end of the field stood a cluster of trees.

Not any old trees. Tullybough trees. Brian's stomach swooped.

He pulled his sleeve forward and rubbed his earring.

'Good of you to call!' squeaked Dulcie. 'I was wondering

when you'd bother. Well, go on then – after him!' Mr Pottigrew had reached the gate. He slid the bolt, pushed it open and walked into the field.

Brian scraped his fingers across his palms. Sweat squeezed under his nails. 'I don't think–'

'Duck!'

Twigs cracked as he shrank into the hedgerow. Mr Pottigrew was turning round. Brian hunkered down and held his breath.

Phew. Whatever the gardener could or couldn't hear, it wasn't him. Breathing out slowly, Brian watched the old man close the gate and set off across the field towards the woods.

'Quick,' Dulcie shrieked, 'or we'll lose him!'

Brian hugged his knees. A nettle brushed the back of his hand. A second of numbness then the sting screamed in. He circled his fingers round the little white bumps bursting from his knuckles. Through the pain came a face, a smile, a scream.

'I can't,' he mumbled.

'Can't what?'

'Go into the woods.'

'Oh.' Dulcie's voice softened. 'I was forgetting. Course you can't.'

Brian's fingers relaxed. Thank goodness. He'd thought for a second there was going to be a scene.

'I mean, imagine if you did go in. You'd actually have to *face* your fear, instead of letting it stew nicely in your memory and ruin your life.'

Brian knew there was something he should be doing right now. Oh yes. Breathing.

'And imagine if we're actually onto something,' she continued. 'I'm sure those missing children would understand that it's *far* too upsetting for you to go in and help them.'

Brian swallowed. Across the field, Mr Pottigrew had nearly reached the woods.

'If I were you,' she said, 'I'd go straight back to Sergeant Poggarty. I'm sure he'll believe you when Mr Pottigrew keeps on acting as deaf as a dustbin, and when he's already been questioned and cleared of suspicion. Why on earth would you bother being brave enough to go in there?' A yawn uncurled into Brian's ear. 'Heroes. They're so last year.'

Two butterflies played kiss-chase above the gate. Mr Pottigrew was at the edge of the woods. Did Brian imagine it or was the old man's back a little straighter? He stepped into the trees and was gone.

Brian stood up. 'You don't understand.'

There's only one thing worse than a sarcastic fossil. A silent one. But no matter how hard he rubbed, there was no reply.

'I can't go into those woods,' he explained.

So why were his feet moving down the path towards the gate? Why were his arms reaching for the latch and his hands sliding it open? Why, when he didn't have a single brave bone in his body, was every one of them acting as if he did?

CHAPTER 16

WHAT'S THE BUZZ?

Scurrying across the field, Brian felt a tap on his head. A drop on his shoulder, a plop on his hand: gentle at first, like a tickle of silver fingers, then harder and faster as the rain got into its stride. And now the whole sky was dissolving, dropping glittering needles down the back of his neck and through his jersey, softening the earth beneath him. Mud spat up his trouser legs as he raced towards the woods, his fear briefly quenched by the drenching.

But under the trees it came roaring back. He leaned against a trunk, itchy and shivering. His jersey steamed sourly. He peered into the gloom. Branches dripped and leaves trembled under the few fat drops that made it through. Splinters of light cracked the shadows. Memories flashed like broken glass. Mum hopping on one leg along the path. Mum hide-and-seeking round tree trunks, picking those tiny blue flowers and sticking them into her brown hurly burly of curls.

'You did it,' peeped Dulcie. 'That wasn't so hard, was it?'

'I'm not going on down there.' Brian nodded towards a track through the trees. Footprints dented the soft earth.

'Why not?' She snorted. 'You've not gone down there for the last two years – and it's hardly helped you, has it?'

The words stung him, sharp and true. The more he'd tried to bury the memory the more it had embedded, breaking the surface only in dreams but twisting and sprouting under every waking hour. There was only one way to root it out.

Have you ever looked at a scab on your knee and just had to pick it, even though you knew it would hurt like a headache in hell? Or turned on the telly to a scary film and just had to keep watching because turning it off would be scarier?

No? Well in that case you won't understand what Brian did next. But because you're smart and kind and a teeny bit nosey, you'll go with him down the path of his nightmares, pushing back branches and brushing wet leaves, until you get–

'There.' He stopped.

Set back from the path, sucking up space and light, was a massive oak. Smaller trees stood at a respectful distance, like courtiers making way for a king.

Brian pressed a hand to his stomach. He couldn't look at it. He couldn't look away. His eyes took him up into branches that wriggled and explored the sky. His feet took him over to the mighty rutted trunk. He reached for a branch above his head.

'I didn't mean *climb* it!' squeaked Dulcie. 'The footprints go that way, along the path. We'll lose Mr ...' She trailed off, as if suddenly realising that this was more important than following the gardener.

Brian pulled himself up into the tree. He remembered every foothold. That knot on the trunk like an old man's knee; that crooked branch above it. Twigs scratched and leaves licked as he climbed into a secret, glass-green world.

'Careful!' said Dulcie as his trainer slipped on wet bark. The higher he climbed the wetter it grew, raindrops sneaking between branches and bouncing on leaves. Another branch, another heave – and there it was. He squashed into a bottom-shaped hollow and looked up.

The branch above him was grooved and wrinkled like rhino skin. Thank goodness for the rain, pressing the tears back inside his eyes. 'That's where she got to.' He pointed at the branch. 'She reached down and tried to help me up. I stretched out my arm and ...'

And what? Did he actually grab her hand? That's what his memory said: that instead of Mum pulling him up, he'd pulled her down. And that Dad, watching from the ground, had never been able to talk about what he'd seen.

But now, looking at the branch, Brian couldn't recall the moment they'd touched. All that came back was the smile, the scream, the snap of a thousand branches. 'I – I can't remember exactly what happened.'

'I can.' Dulcie's voice was strangely gentle.

'What?' He must have misheard. 'You weren't even there. Didn't she take you off to climb the tree? Otherwise you'd have known that she died before I told you.'

'No. I must've blocked out the terrible memory. But now it's coming back.' She spoke more firmly. 'It had been raining and the bark was wet. Your mum wiped her hands on her trousers. That charged me up on her finger. I called out but she didn't hear. I saw your hand reach up as hers went down. But before she touched you she slipped and fell.'

Rain popped on the leaves, little buttons of sound. Brian closed his eyes and tried to remember. But between Mum's scream and that unspeakable crumple on the ground lay a shimmer of silver doubt. Could Dulcie be right?

He pulled off a leaf and crushed it in his hand. 'But Dad. He saw everything.'

'How do you know? Did he tell you? Did you ask?'

'I didn't have to. He's been so sad and polite ever since.

But underneath it's like he's angry, like he blames me for her death.'

'Tell me, what could you see from the ground just now, looking up into this tree?'

'Leaves. Branches.'

'Lots of leaves?'

'Mmm.'

'Lots of branches?'

'Uh-huh.' Brian frowned. Where was this going?

There was a sniff. 'So. You're telling me that you'd sooner believe the imagined report of someone who was standing on the ground and quite possibly looking elsewhere at that moment … someone who you *think*, but can't be sure because you've never actually asked, might have seen you pull – or push, what difference does it make? – your mum to her death through a muddle of green … than the eyewitness evidence of an exceptionally smart, outstandingly attractive bee, who just happened to be sitting on the ring finger of her hand, and who now recalls perfectly the fall that left the aforesaid insect with a sore head and a bruised basitarsus.' She paused for breath. 'And before you ask, that's the proper word for a bee's thigh.' Whether she'd run out of energy or patience, she went quiet.

Brian tried to swallow the hugeness of her words. Could it be true? Could she really have seen it all?

He tilted his head back. Rain soaked his face, sank through his skin and softened his bones. *It wasn't my fault.* The words should be comforting. But they whizzed round his head, crazy and confusing. Over the last two years guilt had become a grim but reliable friend, shaping and guiding his every move. Now it was loosening like the lid on a Coke bottle, leaving him fizzy and dizzy and ready to pop. He looked up. For a second it felt as if the sky was below him: blue-white cracks in a green floor. He closed his eyes and steadied his hands on the rough bark. When the giddiness had calmed he opened his eyes and surveyed the woods from above.

Through the trees, about thirty metres ahead, stood an old cottage. The grey roof tiles, patchy with moss, gleamed darkly as the sun broke through the clouds and the rain began to ease. It was surrounded by a circular stone wall.

Brian had forgotten it was there. But now he remembered walking past it with Mum and Dad. They couldn't see over the wall but had looked through a gap where a gate must once have been into a garden overgrown with weeds and brambles. He'd asked who lived there.

'No one,' Dad had said. 'It's been empty as long as I can remember.'

'Who *used* to live there then?'

Mum had smiled and said, 'Maybe a poor woodcutter

like in Hansel and Gretel. Or maybe a prince who was cheated out of his kingdom by a wicked uncle. Perhaps he fled to the woods to live off nuts and berries because …'

'The uncle was a wizard,' said Brian, 'who'd put a curse on the prince so that every night he turned into a …'

'Woodworm,' said Mum. 'So at least he had plenty to nibble on.'

'Or perhaps,' said Dad, 'it was someone working for the Forest Service who looked after the woods, planting trees and cutting logs and clearing paths.'

'Party pooper,' Mum had laughed, pelting him with leaves. But he was probably right. And now, gazing down from the tree, Brian wondered if maybe Mr Pottigrew had moved in there. Perhaps he had another job after school, tending the woods. The garden certainly looked tidier than he remembered. The weeds had been cleared. There was even a bit of a lawn. And on the far side of the cottage, furthest from the path, was a flower bed.

Brian frowned. With very strange flowers.

They were big, even from this height. To say they bloomed would give completely the wrong idea: their thin oval petals were as grey as dread and their centres were black. At one end of the flower bed stood a white box with a lid. Through the steam rising from the wet leaves it looked as if the box was trembling.

Brian eased himself out of the hollow and climbed carefully down the tree. Jumping the last bit, he stumbled forward. The earth smelled of damp decay. A twig snapped underfoot. The black rags of rooks scattered from a tree. He followed the footprints along the path towards the cottage.

'Shhh,' he hissed. There was a humming in his ear.

'It's not me.'

'What is it then?'

'No idea.' Low and flat, it sounded like a distant chainsaw. Was someone cutting logs? There'd been no sign of that from the tree. His skin prickled. It felt as if the air itself was humming.

The rain had stopped completely by the time he reached the wall. The humming grew louder. It seemed to be coming from the other side. A new smell was rising on the air, thick and sweet. Brian looked further round the wall. The gap that he remembered had been filled by a solid wooden gate. It rose to the top of the wall, about a metre above his head. The gate was closed but the bolt was drawn back. In it dangled an open padlock. *Maybe I can push it open.* He was itching to get a closer look at those flowers.

He walked towards the gate. And stopped. What if there was something, or someone, inside that he really didn't want to see?

As if in answer, there was a squeak. For once it wasn't Dulcie. A bolt was sliding on the other side of the gate. Brian dived off the path. He shrank into the undergrowth, falling backwards into a bramble bush. Thorns bit his arms and snagged his hair. He clamped his lips over the squeal that mustn't escape as the gate opened and Mr Pottigrew came out.

CHAPTER 17

A MAP
AND A TRAP

Brian hunched his shoulders and gnarled his fingers into claws. Maybe if he acted like a bramble he'd look like a bramble.

Mr Pottigrew slid the outside bolt across and snapped the padlock shut. He turned – *oh no* – left onto the path towards Brian. If the gardener didn't actually see him, he was bound to hear his heart booming round the woods like a rock concert. Closer: Mr Pottigrew's boots thudded on the path. Closer: his beard was within tickling distance. Closer: *What will I say? Oh, hi, Mr P. Fancy meeting you here. I was just practising my bramble impressions.*

Brian had always thought that if you could see somebody it meant they could see you too. But either that wasn't true or he'd discovered a talent for bramble impersonation because, to his astonishment, the gardener walked straight past. He carried a small rucksack on his back.

'What's he up to?' he whispered as the old man vanished through the trees, back towards Tullybun.

'One way to find out,' peeped Dulcie. 'Can you climb over that wall?'

Brian felt a flutter of annoyance. It was all right for her, barking out instructions from the safety of his earlobe. 'Anyone could be in there,' he muttered.

'Including Alec, Tracy and Pete.'

'But it might not be safe,' he tried.

'Good point. If it's safety you want, you should go home now.' Brian was beginning to think that was a good idea until she added, 'See you, then.'

'What?'

'I said, see you. Bye. Adios. Toodle pip. Because I'm staying here. *Safe* indeed!' She snorted. 'I've had twenty million years of safe, stuck in this jail of a jewel, and I'm not giving up on an adventure. We're onto something and I'm going to find out what. So before you leave, be a pal and throw me over that wall.'

There's nothing quite so humbling (so I'm told) as being out-braved by someone a thousandth of your head size and two million times your age. It makes you feel a thousandth of their heart size and two million times more wimpy. But only for a moment. Because after that (so they say) you begin to think that if a tiny trapped creature can have that much get-up-and-go without being able to get up and go, then the least you can do is get up and go yourself.

Well, you do if you're Brian O'Bunion.

Standing up, he unhooked the thorns from his jersey and shook the pins and needles from his foot. 'I'm coming with you.' He could have added cuttingly that an amber earring thrown over the wall onto a patch of grass wouldn't be up to much investigating or exploring or adventuring in general. But he wasn't that sort of boy. He did insist, however, on throwing something that *wasn't* Dulcie over the wall first. If anyone was on the other side, surely they'd come out to investigate.

He found a short, thick branch. With his hurliest hurl, he hurled it over the wall. Then he fled across the path into the undergrowth, this time managing to avoid the brambles. He peered out, his heart in his throat, his stomach in his knees and his guts in his elbows.

Nothing. The gate didn't move.

When his internal organs had wriggled back home, he straightened up, crossed the path and examined the wall.

There was a little crack just above knee level. Wedging his foot in, he pushed himself up and grabbed a stone that jutted out above his head. He reached his other hand up to the top of the wall, where jagged stones sat vertically like teeth. He grasped one for a second then lost his grip and thumped down on the ground. He tried again. Again he lost purchase.

'Damn.' The wall was too high and too smooth; there were no other foot or handholds.

'Find something to stand on,' suggested Dulcie. But none of the loose branches or logs lying about was thick enough. It was no good. The wall was unscalable.

Except by Brian O'Bunion.

Feeling for his collar, he pulled off his school tie.

'What are you doing?'

He tied a loop. 'Making a lasso.'

'It's not strong enough. You'll fall and break your–'

But Brian had already wedged his foot in the crack and was gripping the handhold above him. With the other hand, he reached up and hooked the loop round the pointy top stone. Then he leaned back and pulled himself up with the tie.

'Wow,' Dulcie gasped as he clambered on top of the wall. 'Spiderman.' Which he guessed was her way of being impressed.

He half-climbed, half-jumped down into the garden. The humming was louder and the smell stronger, syrupy-sick like lilies soaked in petrol. It coated his tongue and the back of his throat. Crossing the lawn to the flower bed, he pressed a hand to his mouth.

The soil was the colour of wet concrete. The flowers stood in neat rows. Their stalks were as thick as his arm and as high as his shoulder. They bore fleshy grey leaves with silver veins. The tops were like monstrous daisies with grisly petals and black, black hearts.

The humming grew to a low roar, like an approaching motorbike.

'Holy hyacinth!' Dulcie must have jumped in her air bubble because Brian felt his earlobe wobble.

Something was flying towards the flowers. It was coming from the white box that he'd seen from the tree. The box that wasn't a box. And that was trembling not from the rising heat but from the creatures buzzing around it. 'What are *those*?'

For once Dulcie was speechless. Because the word that came closest to describing the furry blobs with fuzzy wings was–

'Bees.' Brian's voice was in his toes. He stared at one of the creatures lumbering through the air. Its body, striped grey and black, was as big as his hand. You'd think its bottom was packed with lead, the way it flew low and almost vertically like a huge furry comma. Its slatey wings sang of exhaustion as it struggled up to a flower and plonked onto the centre. Despite their size the petals shivered, as if even they were repelled by the ghastly guest. An aching disgust rose in Brian's throat. It was all so wrong.

'I can't look,' Dulcie gasped. 'Cover me up.'

Brian pulled hair over his ear.

'Call this evolution?' came her muffled voice. 'What was wrong with us twenty million years ago?'

'Nothing,' Brian whispered. 'You saw Alf's bees. They're just like you. This isn't evolution.'

'So what is it?'

Even if there *was* a word it escaped him because the smell was clogging his brain. He tilted his head to avoid the fumes. Little clouds bubbled in the sky. Imagine dancing up there, a feather on the breeze, nestling into their creamy, dreamy …

'Wake up!' Dulcie stamped a foot in his ear.

He stumbled backwards. 'Sorry. The flowers are making me woozy.'

'Blooming buttercups, this is no time for woozy! We need to check out the house before Mr P. comes back.'

'What if there's someone else in there?'

'What if you check through the window?'

He crept round to the side and peered through the dirty glass. Thankfully the room appeared empty.

Back at the front door, his hand paused on the knob. 'What if it's locked?'

'What if you try it and see?'

There were no more excuses. He turned the cold brass knob.

The door opened. Time took a tea-break as his eyes adjusted to the gloom. Gradually he made out a room. It smelled musty and damp. At the far end was a kitchen area with a fridge, a sink and an oven. The front half was more of a sitting room. Next to a black leather sofa lay a white rug, round and lacy like a paper doily. A lamp stood beside it on a low table. Nothing looked out of the ordinary … except for the wall on the left.

It was covered by a large, unframed map of the world. Photos of faces were stuck on different countries. From each smiling mouth came a speech bubble. 'Wazzup, superdude,' said a boy in the middle of North America. From Spain, a face that was mostly moustache said, 'Hola mi besto!' A South African man did a thumbs-up with a 'Howzit, Q ma bru?' A girl at the bottom of Australia grinned, 'G'day, Number One Unc.' And from Antarctica, a penguin held up a flipper and declared, 'Hey Bro Q, you're cooler than Antarctica.'

Apart from that, nothing seemed out of place … except for the shelves on the right.

They were lined with trophies of every kind. Brian counted thirty-two in all: gold and silver cups, plates and medals, plaques and rosettes. He went over and read the engravings. *National Basketball Champion 1997* said a shiny gold plate. Next to it was a silver tennis trophy for 1999. There were five swimming cups dated from 2000 to 2002. There was a plaque for **Golden Goalie 2003**, and medals and plates for all sorts of games and sports, from chess to ice skating, Scrabble to pole vaulting, and even a cup that said *European Bag Packing Champion 2001*.

'These can't belong to Mr Pottigrew,' murmured Brian. 'He'd never be so good at all those things.' He did a quick – OK, slow – sum in his head. 'And they're all less than twenty years old.' Mr Pottigrew looked about seventy, which meant – after an even slower sum – that he must have been at least fifty when he won them. 'And anyway, if he was so brilliant at everything, why did he end up being a gardener?'

'For which,' added Dulcie, 'I can't see a single award.'

Brian stared at the prizes, trying to make sense of them. Had Mr Pottigrew been the world's most talented fifty-something, then crumpled under the pressure, given it all up and turned to the stress-free art of gardening? Was his deafness a disguise to escape the limelight?

'Hard to believe,' said Dulcie when he suggested it. 'And hard to carry off. You'd think some hint of his talent would slip out.'

Brian pictured the times the football had come Mr Pottigrew's way at break. When Unbeatable Pete had waved for the ball, the gardener's return kick had been anything but golden. As a fellow foot-fumbler, Brian had cringed for him every time.

And even if that had been an act – even if he *was* mega-talented – it didn't explain the map with its photo greetings from all round the world to someone whose name began with Q.

Brian frowned. 'Perhaps this isn't Mr Pottigrew's house. Perhaps he was collecting something from someone called Quentin or Queenie. Perhaps they were out and left it in a rucksack for him, and he had a key to pick it up.' It wasn't very convincing, and didn't explain the freaky garden, but at least it let kind Mr P. off the hook. When it came down to it, his only offence was fake deafness: a little odd, maybe, but hardly a crime.

Brian tried hard to believe it. His suspicions about the gardener had squeezed his insides, made him feel tight and mean. Now he could leave the old man alone to his funny little ear tricks and weird woodland friend.

'Let's go,' he said briskly. He had to get over that wall before Quentin or Queenie or whoever came back. How on earth would he explain his snooping? Besides, there was something about this place – the neat, stale gloom –

that made him want to be somewhere, *any*where, else. He turned towards the door.

'Eeek!'

'Don't do that!' Brian pressed his hand to his ear. 'What is it now?'

'That lamp. By the sofa. It's moving!'

Brian turned back. Cold fingers tickled his spine as he crept over to the lamp. It had looked normal enough from a distance, the shade patterned with butterflies. But now he saw that they weren't patterns at all. They were real. Bright wings fluttered feebly. Their tiny bodies were stuck onto the shade.

'I can hear them,' gasped Dulcie, 'crying and moaning. And, oh, the rug!'

Brian looked down. The white circle was laced with threads that looped and fanned like dozens of joined-up cobwebs. And stuck to the central point of each web was a live – just about – spider. All over the rug, tiny legs twitched in dying semaphore.

'This is torture.' Brian's stomach twisted. What kind of monster would do this for decoration? Bugs they may be, tiny and squashable, with no bigger purpose in life than to scuttle and flutter and lay eggs, but they had nerves which meant feelings and – if they were anything like Dulcie – thoughts and opinions too. To her this must be like a hanging or a crucifixion.

'Do something!' she squealed. 'You've got to help them.'

Kneeling down, Brian peered at a spider in the middle of a lace cobweb. Gently he took the little button body between his finger and thumb and tried to jiggle it free. The creature's legs shuddered, then froze. 'I'm sorry,' he mumbled.

What's that? He bent closer. There was bump near the middle of the rug. He ran his fingertip over a little raised circle. Frowning, he grasped the edge of the rug and pulled it gently away.

It felt like he'd swallowed a watering can.

There was a little metal ring attached to the floorboard. And the fifth floorboard across from it was hinged. *A trap door!*

With shaking fingers he lifted the lid and stared down a flight of wooden steps.

CHAPTER 18

FOUND

Before he had time to remember that he wasn't brave or stupid enough to go down, Brian found himself at the bottom of the steps. The walls either side were made of packed earth. Roots stuck out like electric wires. You couldn't call it a cellar or even a basement; it was too crude, as if a hole had simply been dug in the ground and the wooden steps plonked down. About a metre ahead stood a wooden door. Light escaped round the frame.

Brian stared at the door, his heart a crazy cricket in his chest. A sensible person would turn round. A sensible person would climb the stairs, leave this madhouse and mega-mad garden and go back home, not listen to the fossil in his ear that was telling him to 'Go on, try the handle.'

He licked his lips. A sensible person wouldn't *have* a fossil in his ear.

It's bound to be locked, he told himself. So when the door opened and he practically fell through, it took a moment to steady himself, and a moment more to recognise the faces staring at him, pale and puffy and not entirely unexpected. Because of course, deep down, he'd known they'd be here. It wasn't the usual sort of know that happens beforehand ('I know when I open the door they'll be here') but the slightly cheating sort that comes afterwards ('I knew they would be'). Like the time Sid the Reptile Man visited your school and, the minute he chose someone at random to hold the python, you turned to your best friend and said, 'I just *knew* he'd pick Jamie Doyle.' That was Brian's kind of know. The unsurprising surprise.

What *was* surprising was *their* unsurprise.

'Oh.' Alec was sitting at a desk. 'It's you.' He went back to writing.

Pete was kneeling by the far wall beneath the only two windows in the room. Small and high, they must be at ground level Brian realised. 'Hey, Braino.' Then he went back to drawing on the floor with a piece of chalk.

'What are *you* staring at?' said Tracy from another desk.

It seemed obvious, and perhaps a little rude, to say, 'You.' So instead Brian looked round the room and tried to make sense of what he saw. But the room made the least sense of all. On the left, desks were arranged in rows of three. Alec and Tracy sat in the front row. The other twenty or so desks were empty. All the desks faced to the right. Opposite them, near the right-hand wall, stood another, bigger desk. Above it hung a whiteboard.

It was a classroom. But not just any old classroom – theirs. The desks and chairs were the same as those at school. Along the back wall to the left stood a bookshelf, just the same, and next to it a nature table. Identical posters hung on the walls: rules of the class, geometrical shapes and all the charts comparing pupils. There was a waste-paper bin by the door. There was even a cactus on the front desk.

'What *is* this place?' He gasped.

Silence. He tried again. 'What are you doing here?'

'Writing,' said Alec.

'Drawing,' said Pete from the floor.

'Colouring.' Tracy scowled at him. 'What are *you* doing here?' She wrinkled her nose with such scorn that it took him a moment to remember.

'I'm, uh, here to rescue you.'

Tracy snorted and went back to colouring.

'Rescue?' Pete sat back on his heels. 'From what? We can leave whenever we want.'

Brian was feeling sillier by the second. 'So, ah … why don't you?'

'Duh.' Alec's eyes went wide. 'Because we *don't* want to.' He put down his pen and leaned back in his chair.

Brian blinked round the room. What was he missing? 'Why not?'

It seemed a fair question. But the way the others rolled their eyes, you'd think he'd asked why chickens don't eat eggs.

'Be*cause.*' Alec spoke loudly and slowly, as if talking to someone with very little English. 'We … like it … here. Don't we … guys?' The other two nodded theatrically. Pete put down his chalk and lay on his back, tucking his hands behind his head.

'But your parents, the school, the whole village – everyone's mad with worry!'

Alec stared into space. Tracy coloured in. Pete gazed at the ceiling.

'I said,' Brian shouted, 'they're mad with worry! Don't you *care*?'

Alec's grey eyes settled on him lazily. Then he glanced at his watch. 'Hey, guys, it's nearly tea time.'

'*What?*' Brian scrunched a handful of hair. Missing for days, holed up in this madhouse, families in uproar – and Alec was talking tea time? Had he gone bonkers? Brian ran across the room and grabbed his arm. Talking was clearly pointless. He tried to pull Alec up.

'Get off.' Alec shook him away. He went back to his writing.

Brian turned to Tracy. 'Come *on*. Let's get out of here.' He jiggled the back of her chair.

'Hey.' She glared at him. 'You ruined my colouring.'

Over her shoulder, Brian saw a smudge on an otherwise neat invitation. **YOU'RE INVITED TO MY PARTY**.

'What *is* this?' He circled his forehead with his fingertips. 'Why don't you want to leave?'

Pete sat up. 'We told you. We're waiting for tea.' He hugged his knees. 'Well, not so much tea,' he ran his tongue along his top lip, 'as scones.'

Scones. Why did the word catch in Brian's brain? Why did it burrow and itch like a tick?

He looked at his classmates, lounging in a chair, colouring at a desk and sitting on the floor. They had no intention of leaving; he'd never move them by force, and direct questions were getting him nowhere.

'Wow,' he said carefully. 'I love scones. What sort?'

Tracy's crayon went still. 'Plain, fruit – any sort.' She smiled dreamily. Her eyelids drooped.

Too dreamily. Too droopingly. You'd think she was drunk. Or drugged.

On scones? Since when were they addictive? And who on earth would want to dope the children?

A terrible picture popped into Brian's mind. An old man standing in a doorway with flour on his face. *No.* Surely not

Alf Sandwich, with his gentle ways and thousand kindnesses. Could he really be sneaking into the woods with poisoned teacakes? Brian gripped the back of Tracy's chair. *Never!* Of course it couldn't be Alf. But who, or what, *was* it?

He returned to the door. Rubbing his ear with his sleeve, he whispered, 'Help me, Dulcie.' Her tiny brain was worth two of his; she'd know what to do. There was no answer. For once she must be completely stumped.

He tried again. 'What now?'

More silence.

'Thanks a million,' he hissed.

Alec looked up. 'What for? It's not like we invited you for tea.' He yawned. 'But I guess you can stay if you want.'

'No.' Brian held up his hand. 'Thanks, but I have to go.'

And quickly. Outnumbered by these numb-brains, he could never drag them out by force. His only hope was to leg it back to Tullybun and fetch the gardaí before whoever was behind all this came back.

All of which he was just about to do … when whoever was behind all this came back. Hearing a thump, Brian wheeled round to face the door. Something barrelled into him and he was pushed backwards. Losing his balance, he fell onto his bottom. Pain shot up his spine.

But it was nothing compared to the shriek that shot out of his mouth. 'Mrs *FLORRIS*?!'

CHAPTER 19

AT YOUR SERVICE

There was a tangle of legs, a mangle of arms, a wrangle of boy and teacher. Or rather, what seemed to be teacher. The blue blouse, flowery skirt and sensible heels, from which Brian finally managed to escape, certainly suggested Florrie. But he couldn't be sure because a scarf covered the face.

''Emme go!' it squealed.

Without stopping to think if it was a good idea, Brian leaned over. It took a few moments to undo the knot, thanks to the wriggling head and the wisps of white hair caught in the scarf. After a lot of yanking and shoving – it wouldn't be kind to say that part of him enjoyed the ouches and yowches – the scarf came loose.

'You!' She blinked at Brian. 'And YOU!' She gasped at the others. They looked at her with vague annoyance: the sort of faces *Doctor Who* fans would make when disturbed from the Christmas special by the arrival of a distant uncle with a box of dried figs.

'So.' The teacher glared at Brian. '*You're* involved with this!'

'What?' Brian suddenly regretted untying her hands, which had been bound by rope. 'Of course I'm not, you idiot.' He bit his top lip. Did he really just say that? Did it really feel so good?

Her eyebrows jiggled in outrage. 'How *dare* you–'

'Shut up!' That would've felt even better if it hadn't been accompanied by the sound of a key turning. Pushing past her, he grabbed the door handle. 'No!' He rattled it uselessly. They were trapped.

He turned back to the teacher. 'Who brought you here?' he asked in a flat voice.

'How should I know?' she snapped. 'I couldn't see a thing. One minute I was locking the staffroom door and the next everything went black.' She blew her nose on the scarf. 'Someone grabbed my hands and tied them behind my back. They marched me down the corridor and out the back door. I might've been blindfolded, but I know every inch of my school. Then across the garden and through the trees. They pushed me through the back gate and into a car.'

Pausing to wipe her nose on her sleeve (Brian felt a strange satisfaction at the sight of Florrie-snot), she described the rest of the journey: the car stopping; the door opening; the squelch across muddy ground; the smell of wet woodland; the stumble and tumble into this room.

'Did you hear his voice?' he said.

'Once or twice. "Hurry up, turn left," that sort of thing.' She sniffed. 'And it was high and squeaky. I think it was a she.'

'Or a he in disguise.'

Before Florrie could disagree, a voice sang, 'A he in disguise or a she in disguise? Hee hee, yippee – a *me* in disguise!'

The door flew open once more, whacking into Brian. It was his turn to fall on Florrie. Untangling themselves, they wriggled backwards on their bottoms, staring at the figure who'd come in and was locking the door behind him. He slipped the bunch of keys into his anorak pocket.

'YOU!' Florrie shrieked again. As president of Tullybun's NUASWIALOWD (Never Use a Short Word if a Long One Will Do) Society, she was really letting herself down. 'What are *you* doing here?'

'You?' said Mr Pottigrew, staring at Brian. 'So *you're* the one who left the trap door open.'

'You,' echoed Brian, because he could think of absolutely nothing else to say.

'Me,' agreed the gardener. 'And not me!' He grabbed his beard with one hand and his hair with another. Ripping them off, he threw them across the room. They snagged on the cactus and sat there like vicious candy floss.

'Shot,' said Pete sitting up on the floor. Alec and Tracy clapped from their desks, completely unruffled by the transformation taking place.

The old man in the doorway was shedding years by the second. Underneath the wig his hair was the colour of earwax. He wiped his face briskly with his hands. Wrinkles disappeared, revealing a sharp, pale face. He straightened his back. With a grin and a giggle, the crumbly old gardener was turning into a firm young man. Only his eyes stayed the same, darting from Brian to Florrie in bright blue delight.

The teacher had gone as white as a duck egg. 'YOU!' she gasped – for which she really deserved to be stripped of the NUASWIALOWD presidency. 'I thought there was something familiar about you.'

'But you didn't think hard enough.' The old-young man's voice was indeed high and squeaky. 'All those months of weeding and grovelling, and you didn't recognise your star pupil. Oh dear, Mrs F.' He shook his head sadly. Then he shot forward and shrieked in her face, 'FAIL!'

The teacher yelped. She tried to stand up but he clamped his hands on her shoulders. Brian scrambled to his feet, looking frantically at the other children. Alec was sucking his pen. Tracy was cleaning a fingernail with the corner of a card. Pete doodled on the floor. They seemed amazingly unamazed.

'Who ...' Brian chased the questions playing pinball round his head, 'who are you?'

The man, whose quick, easy movements put him in his mid-twenties, gave a deep bow. 'Quincy Queaze, at your service.'

Somehow Brian doubted that. His mouth opened and closed.

'No need for small talk.' With one hand still grasping Florrie's shoulder, Quincy waved the other breezily. 'I know all about you, Brian O'Bunion. I've been watching you over the year. And it's a lovely surprise to find you here.'

Brian wished he could agree. His eyes strayed to the locked door.

'Who'd have thought? Of all the people to find me out!' Quincy squeezed Florrie's shoulder until his knuckles went white. 'Pretty smart, hey, Teach? Especially for a *lazy loser.*'

'Get your hands off me!' She tried to wriggle free.

He grabbed her wrists. 'You see, Brian,' he said pleasantly, dragging her across the floor to the front desk, 'no one's more welcome than you to my party.' He pulled out a chair behind the desk. 'I know you don't get many invitations.' He plonked the teacher roughly onto the chair and whipped out two pairs of handcuffs from his anorak pocket. 'And I know you've had a tough time at school.' He handcuffed Mrs Florris's wrists to the arms of the chair. 'Believe me, Brian, I understand, because I did too.' He grabbed her neck in the crook of his elbow. 'Didn't I, Teach?'

She tried to duck out of his grip. 'I don't know what you're talking about.'

He clenched her more tightly. 'Oh, I think you do.'

Brian stared at the principal. Her face was going alarmingly red. He really ought to think carefully about seriously considering the different options for perhaps doing something that could possibly help her. But oh dear, not a single option came into his head.

He rubbed his ear. If Dulcie had any ideas, she wasn't prepared to share them, because there still wasn't a peep.

What about his classmates? They didn't look promising. If their expressions were bedclothes, they'd be thin sheets of curiosity over thick duvets of boredom.

Brian had just got past thinking carefully, and was beginning to seriously consider, when Quincy let go of the teacher.

She sat upright in the chair, wriggling her arms. 'This is outrageous!'

'Ooh.' Quincy clapped his hands like an excited toddler. 'Isn't it?' He took a bag from his pocket and put it on the front desk.

Not a bag, thought Brian, staring at the green cloth tube with a zip along the top. *A pencil case.*

'Let me go!' snarled Florrie.

Quincy stuck out his tongue. 'Not on your smelly old nelly.' He unzipped the case and took out a metal ruler. 'I do love stationery,' he sighed. 'So useful and fun. The *only* fun thing about school. You see, Brian –' he waved the ruler in the air, 'I had the same problem as you.' As if a switch had flipped, his face squashed with hatred. 'The teacher!' He tapped Florrie's head with the ruler. 'She really wasn't kind to me.' His eyes widened to sorrowful pools. Like an actor, he seemed to have a wardrobe of faces inside him. 'She was always banging on about how stupid I was. Putting flowerpots on my head to show everyone I was thicker than clay. Calling me Loser, Waster, Fool of the School.'

'That's because you were,' she muttered.

He patted her head with the ruler. 'Fifteen years ago, Brian, I too won a prize. The Melon for Mindless Morons.' Quincy jabbed the ruler in Florrie's chest. 'Remember?'

'Yes, I do.' She glared at him. 'And you deserved every pip.'

'Oh, did I?' He gave what Brian guessed was a laugh, though it sounded more like a lady machine gun. 'We'll see about that, you old scorpion.' Quincy rapped the ruler on the desk. 'Ready folks?'

Pete wiped chalk dust from his hands. 'Yeah.' Stifling a yawn, he pointed to the double white lines that ran round the edge of the floor.

'Excellent,' said Quincy. 'Tracy?'

She nodded listlessly.

'Good. And Alec?'

'Yep.' He put his pen down. 'Hurry up, Quince. I'm staaarving.'

Quince? Brian gaped at the three dozy children who didn't seem the slightest bit scared of this yo-yo of a man whose moods changed like the Irish weather.

'Alec!' barked Florrie. 'Tracy, Pete – what's wrong with you? I *order* you to help me!'

Her prize pupils gazed back, their faces blank as baps.

'Ooh, bossy bossy.' Quincy's eyebrows rose. 'But *I* give the orders round here.' He bent down and pinched her chin between his finger and thumb. 'Because *I'm* the teacher now. And *I'm* going to teach *you*,' he poked her nose, 'a lesson you'll remember,' *poke poke*, 'all your life,' *poke poke poke*.

'You don't scare me,' she growled.

Brian had to hand it to her. For someone forced to sit, she was standing up to him impressively.

'Oh, don't I?' He prodded her cheek with the ruler. She pressed her lips together and sniffed furiously.

Brian rubbed his ear a third time. 'Dulcie!' he hissed. 'You've got to think of something.'

Quincy looked up sharply. 'What?'

'I … I said I was just thinking of something.' Brian smiled nervously.

Quincy chuckled. 'Well, I've been planning something that'll *really* make you grin. Oh, I'm so glad you're here to see it.' He gazed dreamily over Florrie's head, like Dorothy over the rainbow. 'I know you'll enjoy it, Brian. Just like you're enjoying this.' He tickled the teacher's neck with the ruler.

She blinked at Brian. And with a sweet-and-sour rush, he realised that Quincy was right. He *was* enjoying this reversal of power, this bullying of the bully. That was why he hadn't rushed over to kick Quincy's shins and bite his arms, to scratch and pinch and do all he could to help Florrie.

For a moment Brian forgot that he was imprisoned underground, that his classmates had been duped or doped, that his teacher was handcuffed to a chair and that he was the only one who could help them. For a moment he watched enthralled as the failure-hating principal's effort to stop a tear rolling down her cheek scored a big, fat ... F.

Chapter 20

BONKERS AS A CONKER

'You see, Brian, I understand you.' Quincy took a little white bottle from his pencil case. 'Because we're just the same.' He unscrewed the bottle and stood it on the desk. 'Peas in a pod, two flies on a pie.'

Brian's stomach shrank. How on earth could he resemble this freak?

As if he'd spoken out loud, Quincy smiled. His teeth were the colour of custard. 'Not so good at our books. But we notice things. Little things. Creepers and crawlers, scuttlers and squirmers, ants and fleas, beetles and bees. And we love them, don't we? Because we know what it's like to be crushed and downtrodden. We know how a slug feels under a shoe.' He yanked Florrie's ear. 'Remember when you called me Bug Brain for getting three out of fifty in Maths? Or that time you told Pandora Crudge to give me some of her head lice because they'd boost my brain power?'

The teacher stared fiercely ahead.

'Course you don't – because what was it to you?' He frowned at her thoughtfully. 'Hmm. That nose of yours really doesn't work. Shall we try again?' He lifted the lid from the little bottle. With the brush attached to it, he painted her nose white. He tutted. 'Never let us use Tipp-Ex, did you? Said we couldn't hide our failures. Well, you were right. You still look terrible.'

Florrie pressed her lips together.

Quincy danced round to the front of the desk and hoisted himself neatly on top. 'Well, Brian.' He crossed one leg over the other and placed his hands delicately on his knee, like an actress on a chat show. 'All that talk of insects got me wondering.' He changed to thoughtful professor, frowning and scratching his head. 'Are woodlice really so stupid? Are nits truly twits? Tiny, yes, and timid too ... but did you know that there are more than a million species of insect in the world?' He smacked his knee like a cowboy at a hoe-down. 'That there are ten times more termites than humans?' He leapt off the desk. 'There are more kinds of beetles than plants,' he sang. 'Butterflies taste with their feet.' He pranced round the room. 'A cockroach can live nine days without its head. Ants can carry fifty times their own body weight. Did you know –' he skipped back to the desk, 'that insects have lived on this planet *two thousand* times longer than us? Now *that*,' he bent towards Florrie as if to kiss her cheek, 'is what *I* call success.' He blew a gigantic raspberry. 'You may rule the classroom, but bugs rule the world.'

Her face was a fist. 'You're mad,' she muttered.

'As a moth!' He fluttered his arms. 'Which, did you know, use the moon and stars to find their way? Which can sniff each other seven miles away and disguise themselves as –' he leaned over and whispered in her ear, 'poo.' Then he cupped his hands and yelled, 'Pretty smart, *HUH*?!!' As she jerked her head away, he twirled round the desk. 'So.' He stopped in front of it and beamed at Brian. 'I decided to learn from them. I watched them whenever I could: ants carrying crumbs, greenfly on cabbages. I listened to them, talked to them, played Catch the Caterpillar and Hunt the Weevil. They became my closest friends.' He leaned his elbow on the desk. 'Because, Lord knows, I had no others.'

Panic skittered round Brian's chest. *You're right*, he thought. *We are alike*. He stared with horror at his fellow school-hater and insect-lover. *Will I grow up to be like you?*

Quincy grinned. 'And what fine friends they are, Brian. They never insult you, never argue. If you're sad, they listen. If you're angry, you squash 'em. If you're bored, just pull 'em apart.'

Brian felt his earlobe shudder.

'Best of all, they make the perfect snack.' Quincy ran his tongue over his top lip. 'Mmm. Ladybird wings, crisp and spicy. Butterfly heads, chewy as chocolate.'

The shudder spread right through Brian. He pulled his hair forward to protect Dulcie's ears from this Jack the Bug-Ripper.

'You're revolting,' said Florrie.

Quincy reached for the pencil case. He brought out a permanent marker. Grabbing her chin, he drew a droopy black moustache beneath her white nose. 'Look who's talking,' he said sweetly.

The triumph Brian had felt at her humiliation drained away, leaving a scum of disgust and fear. Quincy Queaze was proving madder by the minute.

'So that's why ...' Quincy drew curly ends on the moustache, 'I became a gardener. Chums and yums on tap.' He put down the pen. 'And the prettiest ornaments too.' He pointed to the ceiling. 'Did you see them brightening up my lampshade and rug, Brian? And when they stop moving, I just collect new ones.'

'Monster!'

Brian's left hand flew to his ear. Of all the moments for Dulcie to shriek! And now Quincy was striding towards him. He backed against the door and waited for him to rip out the earring and pop it in his mouth like a butterscotch.

But instead he grasped Brian's shoulders. 'Imagine it.' His blue eyes shone. 'All those suckers under your thumb. You can do what you like and they can't answer back.'

Brian sagged against the door. Dulcie was safe – for now.

'It makes you feel …' Quincy's fingers dug in like tent pegs, 'so powerful. Like – ooh – like a *teacher*!'

He scuttled back to the desk. His right hand closed round Florrie's neck. 'Just as you had fun with me, I have fun with them.' Her eyes bulged like marbles. 'And just like you,' her face was turning purple, 'I have my favourites.' He let go, leaving her spluttering for air. 'Bees.'

Dulcie shrieked again. Brian drowned it in a cough.

Quincy beat a rhythm with his knuckles on the desk. 'Bees are the brightest, bees are the best. Bees knock spots off a ladybird's vest. Clean their bedrooms, nurse their brood, feed their queen on God's own food.'

'Food,' groaned Tracy.

'Yes, yes.' Quincy waved a dismissive hand. 'Coming soon.'

Brian pressed his hands against the door. *Focus*, he told himself. Florrie was fighting from her chair. Dulcie was losing it in his ear. Someone had to keep calm round here. *What do they do in the movies?* His head filled with

Batman, Sherlock, James Bond. *Keep the bad guy talking.* Easier said than done when his mouth was dry as toast, his palms were wet with sweat and his head was buzzing with …

Buzzing with? He caught his breath. 'Those bees,' he said carefully. 'The ones outside. Did you, um … create them?' He swallowed. Quincy was friendly enough now, but any rash word might pop the matey bubble.

Quincy put his palms together and smiled kindly, like a vicar about to preach. 'Brian,' he said softly, 'you are too kind. Create is a word we normally reserve for God.' His eyes rose to the ceiling. 'But, yes, in all modesty I confess they are mine, bred for one single purpose. My beautiful, dutiful,' he turned and roared at the teacher, 'FLORRIBEES.'

Dulcie squealed. Brian fingered his left ear, hoping she'd heed the warning and keep quiet.

'What purpose?' Florrie whimpered. The defiance in her eyes was melting to fear, as if she finally saw the true madness of her captor.

'To teach you a lesson you'll never forget.' Quincy snatched the pen from the desk and wagged it at her threateningly.

'Now!' Dulcie whispered. 'Grab the cactus from the desk, shove it in his face and get the keys from his pocket.'

'No way,' Brian hissed. 'He's too quick for me. And

shut up if you don't want to be eaten.' He tried, and failed, to think of a better plan. *Wrestle him to the ground?* Impossible – he looked far too strong. *Get the others to pin him down?* Dream on. Their brains were as doughy as doughnuts and, besides, they seemed more on Quincy's side than his.

Why? What's he done to them? Brian sensed that the answer held the key to all this craziness. Their craving for scones, those hideous bees and their horrible flowers … what was the link?

An image burned into his brain. A clumsy old gardener in a crowded room. 'The prize-giving!' He gasped. 'You gave Alec and Tracy and Pete those scones. Then you dropped the tray so that no one else would eat any. You drugged them with honey from those bees! That's why they're here and haven't left.' He pressed a fist to his mouth. *Idiot!* So much for speaking carefully. He cowered against the door as Quincy turned to him.

But there was hurt, not anger, in his eyes. 'Oh, Brian, how on earth could you think that?'

Brian swallowed. What was he *supposed* to think about this nutter who redesigned nature?

'I'd never drug these dear children.' Quincy's eyes were bright and warm. 'No, no, I *invited* them. One little taste and they wanted more. So after a while it was only polite to invite them back for tea. And they came, one by one.' He turned to the children. 'Only too gladly, didn't you, guys?'

Alec shifted restlessly in his chair. Tracy licked her lips. Pete bit his cheek. The mere thought seemed to get them drooling.

'And I did nothing to the honey – not me. But it was a good guess, Brian.' Quincy rubbed his hands. 'Ooh, I love a juicy puzzle, don't you? As long as *I* know the answer.' He turned and punched Florrie's arm. 'And *you* don't!'

Brian stared at the man he'd once pitied, now drawing spots on her nose. The man who'd once shuffled from the school hall, shamed and scorned. Who'd now turned the tables, trapping them all like butterflies on a lampshade or spiders on a rug.

Not all. He felt a rush in his chest: a wind that picked up speed, fuelling his fear into action. As Quincy bent over Florrie, Brian took a step towards him. *If I can just …* another step … *creep up behind him …* and another … *and reach into his pock–*

'Hello?' Quincy spun round. Quick as a flame, he darted round the desk and snatched Brian's wrist. 'After my keys, are you?'

Brian's throat filled with sand. *Now what? Will he tie me to a chair? Tipp-Ex my eyeballs?*

He did something far more shocking. Reaching inside

his anorak, Quincy brought out the bunch of keys. 'Allow me,' he said, walking to the door and unlocking it.

Brian blinked at Florrie. She shook her head in bewilderment. The others were too busy dozing to notice.

Quincy opened the door. 'Thanks for coming, Brian. Do pop in again. We'll miss you but never mind. Say hi to your schoolmates and give that crabby old cleaner a kick in the Muttocks from me.'

'Brian!' shrieked Florrie. 'Don't leave me!'

Backing into the doorway, Brian's eyebrows wriggled in code. *I'll get the gardaí and be back in a jiffy.*

Her wail suggested that she didn't speak eyebrow.

And Quincy's grin suggested that he did. 'Oh, and I wouldn't bother coming back. By the time you get here we'll be long gone. It's been lovely to see you, Brian, really it has. But your visit has rather changed my plans. I can't have you fetching the guards and pooping the party I've planned for so long. So I'll just have to take her elsewhere.' Quincy cleaned his fingernail with the key. 'But no worries. Have a great life, Brian.' He waved the key at Pete, Tracy and Alec. 'You too guys. Feel free to leave.'

Tracy lifted her head from the desk. 'After tea.'

'Yeah.' Pete stretched his legs out on the floor. Alec nodded.

'Suit yourselves.' Quincy shrugged in a *what can you do?* kind of way. 'Now,' he said, clapping his hands, 'let's get going.' He unzipped his anorak and threw it on the floor. Then he slipped out of his trousers.

Brian gasped. Florrie yelped. Beneath his gardening gear, Quincy Queaze wore a white shirt, a dark blue tie, grey trousers and a light-blue jersey. He slipped the bunch of keys into the breast pocket, on which were embroidered the words, 'Don't You Know *That*?'

Brian stared at the overgrown Tullybun Primary School pupil. He was crazy as a cucumber, bonkers as a conker – and brilliant. Because what choice had Quincy offered him? To abandon Mrs Florris and save his own skin … or stay here and try to save hers?

Taking a deep breath, he stepped back into the room. 'I'm not going anywhere,' he said softly.

CHAPTER 21

FUN AND GAMES

'How nice you've decided to stay.' Quincy strode past Brian and locked the door again. 'Now where are my manners?' He beamed like a dinner party host while gripping Brian's wrist in a fist you couldn't argue with. 'Do make yourself at home.' He dragged Brian to the desk behind Alec's. 'Please have a seat.' In one graceful sweep he pulled back the chair and pushed Brian into it. 'Time for our first little game.' Humming a happy tune, he scuttled to the front desk and picked up his pencil case.

'What game?' Cement settled in Brian's stomach as he pictured Alec being fixed to the wall with drawing pins or Tracy having her nostrils stapled.

'Oh, just a few questions,' said Quincy airily. 'The sort you get in class. Alec's been teaching me, sharing the contents of his mighty noddle. I can't wait to show our dear teach that I'm not the moron she took me for.'

Brian licked his lips. 'But you left school years ago,' he

said carefully. 'Isn't it time to, um – move on?'

Quincy's face twisted into a snarl. 'You think I haven't tried? I'm telling you, Brian, you'll never escape her words. They'll haunt you forever. Whatever you do, wherever you go, you'll feel useless, pointless, the failure she promised you'd be.'

He might as well have hole-punched Brian's chest. *The failure I already am.*

'Believe me,' said Quincy, 'others will smell your failure like a bee smells pollen. And they'll run a mile, as if it might rub off on them. So you'll have to invent your successes, your own glittering past.' His face went strangely still as if the tiny muscles that worked so hard to disguise and confuse had given up.

Invent your successes? A shock ran through Brian. Those trophies upstairs – they were all phony. Quincy Queaze had rewritten his life.

'But no matter how you try,' sighed Quincy, 'you'll never undo the damage of her words. Only she can do that.'

Florrie squawked from her chair. 'You're brilliant. A genius. There, I've said it. Now let me go.'

Quincy's laugh was drier than a boiled-out kettle. 'If only I believed you. But, oh dear, what a shame, I don't.' He wagged a playful finger at her. 'We'll have no lying in *my* class. Or cheating. I'm going to win fair and square. So you'll see I'm the smartest, most popular and fastest person ever. And you'll be so impressed – so really and truly and deeply impressed – that you'll go back to Tullybun and call a school meeting. And in front of the teachers, the parents, the governors, you'll give me the job that I've longed for all these years.' He whacked her on the shoulder in a chummy kind of way. 'YOURS!'

It's not often that someone's jaw actually drops. But Brian could feel his chin sag and his mouth fall open like a peg bag. *Does he seriously think that'll work? The minute they get to Tullybun she'll have him arrested!*

'And if you think you'll have me arrested –' Quincy wiped his forehead dramatically, 'well phew for my little Plan B. Now, on with the show.' He marched over and sat at the desk next to Alec's. 'I want you to watch closely, Brian. If I don't win fairly, it doesn't count. Ready, Alec?'

Yawning, Alec handed him a sheet of paper.

'Five questions,' Quincy snapped at Florrie. 'And make 'em hard. I've been well trained.'

She gawped at him. 'You can't be serious.'

'Dear me.' Quincy rummaged in his pencil case. 'Such boldness. Some people just don't learn.' He brought out a pair of scissors and rose from his chair.

'No!' squealed Florrie as he came towards her, snipping the air.

'For goodness' sake,' cried Brian, 'do what he says! Five questions.'

A tear rolled down her face. Tipp-Ex spread from her nose to her cheeks. 'What's the square root of one hundred and sixty-nine?' she gasped.

'That's better.' Quincy returned to his chair.

Alec scribbled lazily. Quincy wrote carefully.

'What's the capital of Greenland?'

Alec wrote. Quincy chewed his pen.

'One-fifth plus two–'

'Wait!' Quincy scribbled madly.

'One-fifth plus two-eighths.'

Alec wrote. Quincy wrote and wrote.

'When was the battle of–'

'Hang on!' Quincy crossed out and wrote again.

'Clontarf?'

Alec wrote. Quincy scratched his cheek. Alec sat back. Quincy threw his pen at Alec's foot. Alec bent down to pick it up. Quincy leaned over to Alec's desk.

'Cheat!' Dulcie shrieked.

Quincy spun round. 'What?

Brian coughed. 'You, um, just looked at Alec's answer.'

Quincy's eyes glittered dangerously.

'Sorry,' Brian mumbled. 'It's just that you said no cheating.'

Quincy took the pen from Alec and wrote his answer. 'Collect the papers,' he said coldly.

As Brian took the sheets to the front desk, Dulcie hissed, 'He's madder than a swarm of hornets.'

Brian put the answers side-by-side on Florrie's desk.

'Get me out of here!' she hissed.

What he didn't say:

'Sure, Mrs F, no worries. I'll just push you, handcuffed in your chair, past that nut job armed with lethal stationery, through the door and up the stairs to freedom and a face wash.'

What he did say:

'Make him win. It's your only hope.'

Florrie looked at the sheets in front of her. 'Quincy, five out of five,' she said quickly. 'Alec, nought out of five.'

Quincy tutted. 'Oh dear. I do believe you're lying again. Because I happen to know – though don't ask me how –' he looked sharply at Brian, 'that one of our answers is the same. So Alec must have at least one point, or I must have four points at most.'

Brian gaped at him. He'd insisted on playing fair, then cheated and refused to admit it, then won and refused to accept it! He was changing the rules by the second. How could you reason with someone who had no reason?

'We'll move on,' said Quincy briskly. 'Tracy?'

She lifted her head from her desk and moaned, 'Honey.'

'On its way, I promise. Now, Brian, show these invitations to Teach so she can read them all out. Let's see who's the most popular round here.'

Brian hurried over and took the cards from Tracy's desk. Returning to Florrie, he held up the first card. She gave a manic giggle.

'Read it,' he muttered.

'Dear Quincy,' she said, 'please come to dinner on Thursday. Love Dave.' Quincy smiled from his desk. 'Hey Quincy, hope you can make our barbecue on the twelfth, Rory and Ruth.'

'The twelfth?' Quincy frowned. 'I think I'm at a party that night.'

'Dear Mr Queaze, we would be honoured to have your company at our son Humpty's wedding, from Lord and Lady McDumpty.' Florrie snorted. 'Hey Uncle Quince, please come and stay in July, love Biffy, Ribena and … oh for goodness' sake!' she spluttered. 'I know Tracy's handwriting. These are all made up!'

Just like on the map upstairs, thought Brian. *Imaginary friends.*

'Are not!' Invention must have become second nature to Quincy, judging by the genuine shock on his face. 'They're my friends.'

181

'You? Friends?' Florrie laughed hysterically. 'You've never had friends and you never will. You said it yourself – people sniff you and run a mile. Why? Because failure's a disease without a cure. If you're born with it, you die with it.'

'Shut up,' said Quincy quietly.

But the dam had burst. 'All you can do is infect others,' she yelled, 'including me! Because a failed pupil is the teacher's failure too. Or that's what everyone thinks: the parents, the governors, the school inspect–'

'I said shut UP.' Quincy snatched the scissors and pencil case from the desk.

'Do what you like!' she yelled, her moustache wriggling furiously. 'Snip me or stab me, what difference does it make? You'll still be a failure.'

Quincy rose from his chair.

'Cut off my nose,' she sang as he marched towards her, gripping the pencil case and scissors. 'Slice my ears. Whatever you do, you'll never have friends.'

Oh no. Dropping the invitations on the floor, Brian lunged forward and tried to snatch the scissors. Quincy dodged neatly round the front desk.

Oh no no no. Brian covered his eyes.

But instead of screams there was a stuttering, ripping sound. Brian dropped his hands.

It would have been funny if it wasn't so unfunny. Quincy had fished out a roll of Sellotape from the pencil case and was wrapping it round Florrie's head. 'SHUT UP!' he roared, dancing round her chair, sealing her mouth again and again. 'SHUTUPSHUTUPSHUTUP!'

She did.

When he'd circled her head eight times, he pulled the ring of tape away from her face. She gave a muffled scream as he brandished the scissors. But there was no jab of eyes or stab in the neck, just a clean snip of the tape. Quincy clearly hadn't finished with her yet.

Letting out a slow breath, Brian sank down at the desk next to Alec's.

'There,' said Quincy pleasantly, patting Florrie's wraparound mouth. 'No more talking in class.' He put the tape and pencil case on the front desk and smiled at her, calm as cream.

If someone had said four hours ago that Mrs Florris was going to be Tipp-Exed out, coloured in, whacked by a ruler and wrapped in tape, Brian would have bought popcorn and a front row ticket. But now, as he stared at the polka-dotted, moustachioed, Sellotaped, snivelling prisoner, something dark and treacly rose up his throat and sat in his mouth that tasted astonishingly like pity.

Quincy grabbed a fistful of her hair. 'And you're wrong,

dear Teach. I *do* have friends.' He snipped off a white clump
and sprinkled it over the floor. 'These lovely children for
starters.' He waved the scissors at Alec, Tracy and Pete. 'They
could have left any time but they chose to stay.' He snipped
and sprinkled another white curl. 'If that's not friendship,
what is?' Snip. 'And Brian here's my besto.' Sprinkle. 'Aren't
you, Brian?' Snip and sprinkle.

Brian nodded, clearing his throat to mask the snort from
Dulcie. As long as Quincy believed that, there was a chance
of persuading him to let them all go. Or forcing him. *If I
could get hold of those scissors, maybe I could threaten him.*
At last Quincy laid them on the front desk, though not
before prodding the tip of the teacher's nose.

'Now for our last little game.' Quincy clapped his hands.
'Ready, Pete?'

Pete dragged himself up from the floor. He stood on the
outside of the double line he'd drawn round the room.

Quincy stood level on the inside line. 'On your marks,'
he cried. 'Get set–' He took off round the track. Then he
called back over his shoulder, 'Go!' He waved at Brian. 'Ten
laps. Start counting.'

'One,' called Brian, as Quincy legged it round the shorter
circuit while Pete ambled slowly and inaccurately along the
outer line.

'Two to Quincy.'

Pete stopped to rub his eyes.

'Three to Quincy.' Brian rose slowly from his desk. 'One to Pete.'

Pete yawned.

Brian pushed his chair backwards. 'Five to Quincy.' He took what he hoped was a casual step towards the front desk. 'Two to Pete.' And another. 'Eight to Quincy.' A few more. 'Four to Pete.' He reached out what he hoped was a relaxed arm. 'Ten to Quincy.' His fingers closed round the scissors.

'Thank you thank you,' panted Quincy, throwing his arms out and continuing to run like an Olympic hero before an adoring crowd. 'And thank *you*.' Trotting past Brian, he snatched the scissors from his hand, then the pencil case and cactus from the front desk. 'You won't be needing those.' He lifted the desk lid, threw all the potential weapons inside and slammed it down. Then, with a twist and a hop, he popped his bottom on top of all hope.

CHAPTER 22

NUMS FOR CHUMS

'Oh, Brian.' Quincy leaned forward on the desk. 'Why did you want those pointy things? I'm not going to hurt you.' He winked. 'We're pals, remember?'

Brian nodded madly and made loud 'Mmm' and 'Yesss' noises, partly so he could think up an excuse for trying to grab the scissors, and partly to drown out the snorts of derision he expected from Dulcie. But none came. Thank goodness; she must have run out of puff. And thank badness, too, because now he was on his own. 'I was just going to cut the tape from Mrs Florris's mouth so … she can congratulate you for beating Pete. And if you undo the handcuffs, she can clap too.'

'Ooh, wouldn't that be nice?' said Quincy sweetly. 'But she had her chance.' He twisted round on the desk to face her. 'And she blew it.' He cuffed her on the ear.

The loathing in her eyes suggested that she wasn't in the mood for congratulating. Brian would have to do it for her. 'You were brilliant,' he told Quincy. 'You beat the unbeatable. Didn't he, Pete?'

'Whatever.' Pete had collapsed into a chair. 'Where's my honey?'

'Yeah.' Alec's head rose from its slump on his chest. 'You promised.'

'I did indeed.' Quincy jumped off the front desk. 'And seeing as Teach hasn't played ball, it's time for my little Plan B. A trade-off. In return for some of my delicious, nutritious honey, she'll be only too glad to give me her job.' He took the keys from his breast pocket. 'She's a lucky woman. I tell you, Brian, it's irresistible.' He locked the lid of the desk. 'In fact, you must try some too. I'd hate you to feel left out.' He skipped to the door, ran out and slammed it behind him. There was the creakety-squeak of a key.

Brian's chest went tight. He'd lost his last weapon against Quincy. Trust.

Or maybe his last-but-one. He ran over to Florrie. 'Hold still,' he muttered, running his fingernail along her taped mouth. He found the end of the tape by her ear. 'If we're going to get out of here, you've got to flatter him, say what he wants and make him believe it. It'll only work coming from you.' He ripped off the sticky bandage. Tears glittered on her cheeks. She squeaked and gasped as the tape plucked white hairs from the back of her head and burned a red line across her face.

'Aoww,' she moaned, wriggling her moustache back to life. 'You hurt me.'

'Sor*ree*,' snapped Brian. 'Just do it right this time, OK?'

The door opened. Quincy swept in with a tray. On top was a spoon and a glass jar of something mottled yellow and grey. He locked the door. Lifting the tray above his head, he glided across the room like a waiter, ten days and a world away from the clumsy old klutz in the school hall. 'Num nums for chum chums!' he sang, putting the tray on the front desk.

Brian backed towards the door. Alec, Tracy and Pete rose from their chairs and hurried slowly (it *is* possible: imagine running through ketchup) towards him.

'*Oh* no.' Quincy snatched up the jar. 'Guests first.'

You had to hand it to him. For a kidnapping, mind-mangling, stationery-wielding nutcase, he had lovely manners. Either that or he was enjoying the children's agonised faces as he shoved them away. 'If you don't wait nicely, you won't get any at all. Go and sit down.' They slunk wretchedly back to their desks. He put the jar down on the front desk. Seeing Florrie's untaped mouth, he frowned. 'Now, Brian, why did you go and do that? I thought you'd be glad that I gagged the old hag.'

'Yes.' Brian dug his fingernails into his palms. 'But like I said, she wants to congratulate you on beating Pete.'

'Congratulations,' said the teacher flatly.

'And tell you how clever you are.'

'Clever,' she agreed.

'And how wrong she was, and how sorry she is for making you feel so useless at school.'

'Wrong,' she said dully, 'and sorry.'

'Gee.' Quincy's hands clasped his cheeks. 'What super, super words.' He sighed. 'If only she meant them. It's kind of you to try, Brian, it really is, but you can't change her.' He smiled. 'Now, you just relax and enjoy a nibble of my finest.' He took the spoon and plunged it into the jar of ghastly honey. 'I normally serve it on scones,' he chirped. 'You don't need much; it's powerful stuff. But for you I'll spare a whole spoonful, so you can savour the enchanting flavour.'

'NO!' Brian flattened himself against the door. One taste and he'd be done for. 'I – I'm allergic to honey.'

'Really?' Quincy stirred the yellow-grey goo. 'Even better. It's been such a hit with the children, you see, I'm thinking of selling it. And I was wondering how it would work on people with allergies.' He pulled the spoon out. 'You'll be my test case, Brian. Oh, it's all working out so well.'

With his hands behind his back, Brian pressed

pointlessly on the locked door handle. His sweating palms slid off the cold metal. 'What's *in* the honey?' he whispered.

'Aha!' Quincy patted the pot. 'The secret ingredient. How do I know you won't go and blab it?'

'Because,' Brian swallowed, 'like you said, I'm your friend. And friends never blab. They can trust each other.'

'They can?' Quincy frowned.

'Yes. They keep each other's secrets ... and they never hurt each other.'

Quincy's rusty eyebrows rose. He seemed to be listening at last.

The other children seized their chance. Rising from their chairs, they rushed sluggishly (it can be done: think of running through mustard) towards Quincy.

Who snatched the jar and jumped on top of the desk. 'Iron!'

'Iron?' echoed Brian. 'What do you mean? I don't see–'

'Oh but you do. Seeing's what you're good at, Brian, like me. Noticing things that other people miss.' Quincy held the pot high as the children jostled beneath him. 'I've spent years watching bees in gardens, studying their ways. How they talk, not in words but the language of nature – colours and smells and touch. Did you know,' he did a jig on the desk, 'that flowers attract bees through magnetic waves? And if bees can be magnetised, why not us too? Through their honey.'

'Honey!' moaned Tracy grabbing his trouser leg. He kicked her away.

'But why do you want magnetic honey?' Brian flattened his hands against the door. 'I mean, what would you use it for?'

Quincy grinned. 'To settle a sticky old score.' He bent over and banged the pot on Florrie's head. She shortened in the chair like a hammered nail. 'One day in the garden it all came together in a single, beautiful word.'

Kidnap? Torture? Brian's mouth filled with dust. *Murder?*

Quincy kissed the honey pot. 'Fertiliser! Magnetic soil, magnetic flowers. Magnetic nectar, magnetic pollen. Magnetic bees, magnetic honey. I told you I put nothing in the *honey.* I just magnetised the iron in the fertiliser and let nature do the rest. And the result has simply captivated these dear, gifted children.' He stamped on their hands as they clutched at his feet. 'See? They can't keep away.'

Magnetic fertiliser. That was why the soil, the flowers, the bees outside looked so … *metallic.* But Brian still didn't get it. 'Why go to all that trouble? Why not just kidnap the prize-winners and force them to teach you their skills?'

'Kidnap?' Quincy's eyes widened. 'What sort of monster do you think I am? I wasn't out to use them. I wanted to be friends. So I gave them a present … a little encouragement. And then they *chose* to come, like friends do.'

'You're as loopy as a Hula Hoop!' screeched Florrie. 'As nutty as Nutella!'

Oh no. Brian sank to the floor. *She's lost it. We're lost.*

'That's not friendship!' She cackled like a chicken. 'It's bribery.'

Quincy's eyebrows rose. 'Bribery?' He licked his lips, as if exploring a new and intriguing taste. 'Do you really think so?'

'No!' cried Brian, and 'I *know* so!' yelled the teacher.

Quincy hugged the honey to his chest. 'But I thought they were my friends,' he said, all round-eyed innocence. He gazed down at the three children, shoving and smacking and trying to grasp the pot. 'You're right, though.' He tutted. 'It really does look like it's the honey they're friends with, not me.'

'Ten out of ten!' Florrie laughed hysterically. 'For once!'

Quincy kicked out with his foot, hitting Alec in the face. 'Well, forget it, you fakes! I'm saving it for my *real* friend.' He jumped off the desk and strode towards Brian, holding the honey jar above the others' clawing reach.

'No!' Brian covered his mouth with his hand and squashed against the door. 'If you give me that honey, I *won't* be your friend. I'll just be your slave, like the rest of them.'

Quincy stopped. 'You will? Oh!' He blinked uncertainly.

'I … I see what you mean.'

As he hesitated, Tracy leapt for the honey pot. But again he was too quick, dodging and jumping onto a chair. Alec grabbed his knees. Tracy wobbled the back of the chair. Pete kicked the legs. Quincy came clattering down – but not before he'd hurled the honey pot at one of the windows. The glass cracked, scattering stars as the jar and spoon smashed through. There was a thud on the ground outside.

With a cry, Pete dragged a chair across to the wall. Alec and Tracy followed.

'Who needs honey?' Quincy danced to the front desk. 'Now I've got a *proper* friend!'

From the door, Brian watched Pete climb onto the chair and reach up to the broken window. But it was too high to stick his hand through.

There was a shriek from Florrie. Quincy had unlocked the lid of the front desk and taken out a matchbox. He struck a match and dropped it into her lap.

Brian's brain froze. But his body thought for him. He flew across to her.

Quincy darted past, sweeping up the anorak he'd thrown on the floor. 'Time to replace the queen bee,' he sang, skipping to the back of the room. 'Come on, Brian, let's smoke her and her little workers out!'

Reaching the front desk, Brian flicked the match from

the screaming Florrie's lap. Too late. A flame had caught the bottom of her blouse. He grabbed it, smacking and squeezing the burning cotton. Pain ripped across his palms. Tears stung his eyes. At last the flame died, leaving the end of her blouse in tatters and his hands in roaring agony.

At the back of the room Quincy was crouched at the foot of the bookshelf. He'd thrown down the anorak and was dropping burning matches on top. Flames rose, timidly at first, then thickening as they ate through the lining to the padding. As Brian rushed back between the desks, Quincy turned to the nature table. He scooped everything off the top – bark, moss, dried flowers – and threw it on the flames.

Brian reached out and tried to snatch the matchbox. '*Owww!*' Pain tore his hands.

Quincy wheeled round and gripped his wrists. His eyes were wild with joy. 'Let's make 'em sizzle!' Dropping Brian's wrists, he struck another match. Brian charged again but Quincy flicked him away like a fly. He tumbled onto the floor. Quincy seized a book from the shelf, ripped out a handful of pages and threw them on the anorak. The flames crackled and danced, orange as egg yolk.

Brian clutched at Quincy's trouser leg. But his throbbing fingers had no strength. Quincy skipped off and pulled more books from the shelf. He threw them onto the fire, cackling.

'Help!' Brian yelled pointlessly. The other children were still trying to retrieve the honey. They'd dragged a desk to the wall. Pete stood on top, reaching for the window. Florrie was sobbing in her chair.

Brian struggled to his feet. It was hopeless tackling Quincy alone; he was far too strong and quick. As he capered towards the door, Brian focused instead on the fire. He grasped the bottom of his jersey. *Aaaah!* His fingers felt shrunken and tight, as if he'd dipped them in molten wax. Dizzy with pain, he wrenched the jersey over his head. Then he whacked it at the flames. Ash flew up and stung him like ants. Smoke rose and spread across the ceiling, then curled down and out through the broken window.

Pete coughed in the fumes. He gave up, sank down and slid off the desk. The three children turned. They looked at Brian with bleak, defeated eyes. But seeing Quincy at the door, their daze turned to desperation.

'Honey!' wailed Alec. They stumbled towards him between the desks.

Quincy was dropping burning matches into the bin by the door. As the contents caught fire, he threw flaming balls of scrunched-up paper at the children. Then he caught sight of Brian still hitting the flames. 'What are you doing?' he cried, as if understanding only now that Brian was fighting, not helping, him. 'Leave those losers and save yourself.' He opened the door. 'Come with your real friend, Brian.'

Brian came ... not with but *at* him. He rushed towards the open door and hurled himself against Quincy, knocking him sideways. 'Now!' he yelled to Alec, Tracy and Pete. 'Get out of here!'

But as they reached the door, Quincy regained his balance. He threw Brian towards the children, sending them all sprawling backwards. 'You traitor!' he screamed. 'You had your chance! You can fry with the rest of 'em.' And with that, the grey-trousered, blue-jerseyed, school-mottoed maniac was gone. The door slammed. The key creakety-squeaked in the lock.

CHAPTER 23

HOTTING UP

Alec, Tracy and Pete stared in horror at the door. Then they sank to the ground, their last hope of honey in tatters. Brian looked round wildly. The fire at the bookshelf was gaining strength. Smoke was thickening quickly below the ceiling. They had minutes left to act before it sank and filled their lungs.

Or rather he did. The honey-starved children were no use at all. 'Get back to the window!' he ordered. 'And keep low.' At least that would buy them more air and time while he thought of something.

But what? *If I smash the other window, more smoke can escape. But the extra air will feed the flames.* Panic clouded his brain. He couldn't think straight. He needed help.

'Dulcie!' He raised his left arm, brought his shirt sleeve to his ear and rubbed like he'd never rubbed before.

'Stop the fire first!' she shrieked. 'Use the trousers!'

Brian seized the gardening trousers still lying by the

door and rushed back to the bookshelf.

Over and over he smacked at the flames, trousers in one hand, jersey in the other, his eyes stinging from the heat, his hands from the pain and his throat from the smoke that scratched with vicious fingernails. He kicked books away from the edge of the pile, coughing and spluttering.

'That's it!' squealed Dulcie. The flames shrank under the heavy fabric of the trousers as he pounded with a strength scooped from nowhere. 'You've done it!' The last flame flickered and died. 'Now smash the other window! You have to get rid of the smoke.'

She was right. But there was something else he had to do first. The children were lying on the floor by the window where the last clean air lingered. But Florrie was higher, still sat in her chair, her head shrouded in smoke. If Brian didn't get to her, the fumes would.

'I said the window!' peeped Dulcie as instead he snatched up an unburned book from the floor and crouch-ran to the front desk. He lay on his back, raised his legs and pushed the chair over with his feet. The gasping Florrie toppled onto her side.

Wriggling on his bottom and still clutching the book he elbowed and shouldered a desk to the wall below the other window. He took a deep gulp of precious air and hauled himself onto the desk. He staggered to his feet. Smoke stuffed his nose like boiling carpet. He raised his arm and flung the book at the window. It smashed through the glass and thudded outside.

Shot, he thought vaguely as his brain began to melt.

Good, he thought dimly as smoke billowed through the hole.

Nothing, he thought blankly as he crashed to the ground.

CHAPTER 24

THE FLIGHT

When you haven't stretched your legs for a while, they can feel a little stiff. And when your wings have been clipped and your living room cramped for a good few million years, it takes time to adjust to freedom.

But time was something Dulcie didn't have. And freedom was proving scary. It wasn't just the jolting shock as Brian's head hit the floor ear-first. Or the heat that struck as the amber cracked around her. It was more than the sour stench, coiling smoke and wicked fumes that made her antennae flinch. It was Brian.

Or rather the lack of him. Taking her deepest breath for twenty million years, she yelled, 'Wake up!'

No response.

Standing on the amber shards, she stuck a feeler into his ear.

Not a twitch.

She lifted a front leg, greeting each muscle as it rippled

200

into life. When all six legs had rehearsed, they performed together, a tiny orchestra of movement that carried her over the shattered amber. She crawled round the rim of Brian's ear and across his cheek. Reaching an eye, she wedged her antennae underneath the wiry lashes.

His lid didn't budge.

She stopped to catch her breath. *My breath! I'm alive!* All that fear of freedom – all that refusing to let Brian crack the amber – what a waste. Because here she was, alive and almost kicking, while the children gasped for breath and Brian lay there unconscious or …

No! She crawled down the scorched red ridge of his nose. Perching on his upper lip, she stuck a feeler up each nostril. *Thank goodness.* Her antennae swayed gently in the darkness between crusty, singed hairs. He was still breathing. But for how long?

She pulled out her feelers and fluttered her wings. *Come on, Dulcie!* She tensed her shoulders and fluttered again. The hairs on her abdomen trembled in the draught. *You can do it.* She flapped her forewings and twisted her hind wings. *Harder.* Flap and twist. *Again.* Flap-twist. *That's it.* Flap-twist and … *lift off*! With a mighty gasp she was flying through the stinking smoke, up the wall and out through the window hole. She collapsed on the ground, trembling from head to sting. *I haven't got the puff. I can't do this.*

Can't wasn't an option. Brian was dying. Time for some flying.

Where to? The police – then what? A buzz round their heads, a squeak in their ears? Even if she had the breath, they'd swat her before she could open her mouth – and so would everyone else in Tullybun.

Hang on. Not everyone.

She sniffed. They'd never be up to the job.

But if not them, who?

Wiggling her wings, Dulcie eased herself into the air.

Oh, thank you, breeze! Like a breathy hand it scooped her up and along.

Oh, thank you, trees! They rustled their leaves, cheering her on like a crowd at a race.

Oh, thank you, sun! The evening light slanted into her, a solar sat nav that bypassed her mind and led her muscles out of the woods, across the field and back to Tullybun.

*

Jan looked up from her sweeping. There was someone at the door. She could smell it: a musty, dusty, unfamiliar scent. She froze. Who could it be? She crept towards the entrance, the hairs on the back of her neck stiffening. The smell grew stronger. She peeked through the doorway.

Phew. The guards were there, weapons aimed, interrogating the stranger.

And what a stranger she was! A jumble of contradictions: fully formed but tiny; laden with food but underfed. Not a wasp, not a hornet, definitely not bumbly, but hardly a honey bee either.

Claire and Louisa joined her at the door. Sue and Beyoncé followed. Her sisters were abandoning their work, buzzing to the entrance to see the action, nudging their wings and wiggling their feelers for a better view.

The tension in the air turned to excitement. The weary visitor didn't look much of a threat. And her hind leg bulged with the biggest bag of pollen Jan had ever seen.

The guards lowered their bottoms. Turning round, they aimed their stings *inside* the hive, telling the crowd to make way.

The sisters bowed their heads and cleared a path for the guest who'd come to guide them to a feast. Leonora pointed her feelers towards a cell full of honey, inviting the visitor to feed. But the tiny bee shook her head and crawled into the clearing, desperate to start her dance.

Left and up at fifty degrees, wiggled Dulcie's bottom. *Left and up at forty degrees. Right and across at thirty degrees.* She shimmied as if there was no tomorrow – which for Brian there might not be. *Down at a hundred and eighty degrees.*

Her mind might be fuzzy but her butt was as clear as a summer's day. *Left and up again, fifty degrees.* She poured herself into the dance of a very long lifetime.

But it wasn't the dance she'd dreamed of for twenty million years. Instead of flowers and food, it spoke of fire and fumes and trapped bodies. A horrified buzz ran through the audience as they learned how life was slipping from their master's beloved friend. They had to help Cap'n O'Bunion. But how?

As Dulcie waggled the answer, a ripple ran through the crowd. It was bold. It was brilliant. But it needed a leader.

Not this strange little bee from the blue. Finishing her desperate dance, her legs gave way and she collapsed on the comb.

Leonora rushed to the honey-filled cell. She scooped the sticky paste onto her tongue and scurried back. While Sue and Sadie pried the stranger's jaws apart, Leonora pushed the honey into her mouth. There was a twitch of legs and a flutter of wings. Then the little bee went still again.

Maybe I was wrong, thought Dulcie faintly. *Maybe, just maybe, they* can *do the job.*

In the crowd Jan sniffed. A new smell crept into the air: heavy and rich, noble and kind. The queen was agreeing to share her food.

A lady-in-waiting bustled through. Lowering her head,

Nurse Nessa thrust her proboscis into the guest's tiny mouth. On the tip was a blob of royal jelly. If that vitamin-stuffed, energy-boosting, royal supersnack couldn't revive her, then …

All heads turned. The queen herself was arriving. Not in her usual stately procession, flanked by bodyguards and cleaners, hairdressers and leg waxers, but alone. Her Royal Humness Queen Beatrice had accepted the mission.

Crawling to the entrance and spreading her wings, Queen Bea led her girls from the hive.

*

Alf shuffled into the kitchen, his slippers smacking on the tiles. Yawning, he crossed to the fridge. Time for his night-cap, the hot milk and honey that always helped him sleep.

His hand paused on the door. Funny. The dear old fridge he'd refused to change since Elsie died was buzzing more loudly than usual. He peered inside. Nothing. And come to think of it, the buzzing was coming from behind. Taking out the milk bottle, he turned round.

And dropped it.

'Alice?' he gasped. 'Katie? Gladys, Sadie … Charlotte, Jan … *Queen Bea*?' His hands flew to his cheeks as they swarmed through the window faster than he could name them. 'What is it?' They buzzed and flurried, haloed his head, tickled his ears, mumbled and muttered, crowded and clouded. 'Calm down, girls. Tell me what you want.'

They did. Forming an arrow-shape, with the queen at the tip, they flew down the hall. Alf tied the belt of his dressing gown and hurried after them. 'Come on then,' he said, opening the front door. 'Where are we going?' The bees hung in a dark cloud while about thirty broke off and buzzed back inside. They landed on his mobile on the hall table. 'All right, all right.' Alf picked it up and slipped it into his dressing-gown pocket. 'Happy now? Lead on, Queen Bea.'

*

Mrs Fripp squealed. It wasn't at the blob of chewing gum that she'd just spotted on the lamp-post during her evening patrol. It wasn't at the Wrigley's wrapper that had missed the dustbin and was shimmering on the pavement in the dying light. It wasn't even at Anemia Pickles who, on her way home from work, was pressing – yes, *pressing* – a piece of gum onto a fence post. In fact she was squealing too. 'What the bleedin' 'ell is *that*?'

'Keep back.' Mrs Fripp grabbed Anemia's arm and pulled her behind the lamp-post. 'Alf's bees are swarming. They must be looking for a new home. Leave them to him. He'll catch them when they land.'

But they didn't. In a rare moment of harmony, the founder of the 'Tullybun Says No to Gum' campaign stood arm in arm with the village's greatest gum-chewer, gawping at the little old man who'd turned right off High Street in pursuit of the buzzing cloud.

'Slow down,' he panted. But they were already at the far end of Gandhi Way.

'Give us a sec,' he puffed as they veered left into Joan of Arc Street, then right down Spartacus Lane.

But as they buzzed across the field and into the woods, he began to understand that there wasn't a sec to be had. And when they led him through the gate in the wall, which some hasty person had forgotten to padlock, he started to think it was a matter of life and death.

And as he rushed to the side of the house, where smoke was curling from two holes at the bottom, and shone the light of his mobile through, he began to doubt the life bit.

'Fire,' sobbed Alf into his phone. 'Tullybough Woods, cottage by the path. Kids here. Quick.'

CHAPTER 25

NO!

Everything was one big ouch. His arm when he tried to lift it. His toes when he ventured a wiggle. His nose, his shoulders, his elbows – even his eyelashes. *Can eyelashes hurt?*

Oh boy and how! They scraped like scouring pads as he blinked awake. His eyes smarted in the clean white light.

Smarted. What a word. *At last I'm smart.* Brian tried to smile. It felt as if his cheeks were cracking.

'Brian?' Dad's face was in his face. 'BRIAN?'

'Ow,' said Brian as a tear landed on his forehead.

'Ow?' said Dad. '*Ow?*'

Alf's face joined Dad's. 'Ow?' he cried. 'OW!' If they were trying to make conversation, Brian wasn't impressed. 'You're back, Cap'n! You're with us!' Alf saluted. 'Aye blessed aye!' Another tear fell onto Brian's nose.

'Ow,' he said.

'OW!' yelled Dad.

'OW OW!' sang Alf.

Brian would roll his eyes if they weren't so sticky, and if he wasn't beginning to realise that he'd actually survived that living nightmare of heat and smoke and pretty much hell. No wonder it felt as if he'd been stung by a zillion bees.

Bees? It all came crashing back. Quincy Queaze, the cellar-cum-classroom, Florrie, his classmates and … 'Dulcie!'

'Dulcie?' said Dad, smile-frowning over him.

'Dulcie?' said Alf, stopping his rumba round the room.

'I mean – my earring.' Brian tried to lift his hand. *Big screaming ouch.* He dropped it.

Dad raised his eyebrows at Alf in a *what's-he-on-about?* kind of way.

'The bee,' said Brian. 'Is it still inside?'

'No. Why?'

And now it was Brian who was crying, except that his tears were all dried out. So he had to make do with little rhythmic sobs like the rasp of a handsaw. That got Dad and Alf crying again and reaching over to hug him as gently as they could.

'She must've died in the fire,' whispered Brian.

'No,' said Dad. 'She's OK. And the children too. They're all recovering along the corridor.'

'I don't mean Florrie.' In a parched whisper, Brian told them about the tiny friend who'd bossed and encouraged him, coaxed and cajoled – who'd stuck by him, literally, until the end.

Dad's mouth was a perfect O.

Alf's mouth opened, then closed, then opened again. 'Except,' he said at last, 'that she didn't.'

'Didn't what?'

'Stick by you. I was wondering how my girls knew where to find you. She must have escaped from your ear, flown to their hive and waggled your whereabouts.'

Never mind the pain, never mind the shattering of a thousand cheek cells, Brian's grin was wider than his face. 'She must be there now. Go and get her, Alf.'

'Aye aye, Cap'n.' Saluting, Alf hurried out the door.

Dad drew his chair closer to the bed. 'Brian.' He sat down. 'I know I've not, ah, been the best dad. I've been so caught up in myself since …' he took a deep breath, 'since your mum died. I thought nothing worse could ever happen.' He cleared his throat. 'But it did, almost. What I'm trying to say –'

And making a right cowpat of it, thought Brian.

'Is that when I look at you I see her. And up until now that's been … hard. But now … now that I nearly lost you too, I'm so, so grateful.'

'It's OK.' Excitement bubbled in Brian. He tried to sit up, winced and sank back on the pillow. 'I know you think that I made her fall. That I pulled her from the tree. And I thought so too. But it's not true.'

Dad frowned.

'You couldn't see properly from the ground. And I couldn't remember. But Dulcie could. She was right there on Mum's hand, and she saw everyth–'

'No,' said Dad softly.

'What?'

'She was in my pocket.'

Brian's chest iced over.

'Your mum asked me to look after the ring while she climbed. Dulcie didn't see a thing. And I – I did.'

He said no more. He didn't have to.

'So I did kill her.' Brian's voice was flat.

'*What?*' Dad looked as if he'd been punched in the face. 'Of course you didn't! Is that what you've thought all this time? Oh, my dear, dear …' he looked wildly round the room, as if in search of the right word … 'dear.' He shook his head. 'And when I was so distracted and sad, you thought I was blaming you for a terrible, terrible accident that was nobody's fault.'

Brian swallowed. 'Nobody's?'

For the first time in two years, one month and twenty-nine days, Bernard O'Bunion looked – really looked – at his son. 'Nobody's fault at all.'

*

It was the oddest weather forecast. Despite the warm front, Sharlette Briquette looked as if she'd been in a hurricane. Her hair was a haystack. Her lipstick danced over her cheeks. Her blouse was creased, her brooch upside down.

She *had* been in a hurricane. And now it was over. 'My Tracy's OK!' she shrieked at the camera. 'She's talking and eating. She's charming the pants off doctors and demanding more pocket money. What do I care if the rain falls in Spain or what's blowin' in the wind? The sun has got his hat on and he looks like this!' The camera panned to the weather chart. And instead of little suns indicating fine weather over Ireland, there were little Brian O'Bunions.

'Turn it off, Dad.' Sitting up in bed, Brian blushed. As Dad pressed the TV remote, there was a knock at the door. Alec, Tracy and Pete shuffled in. Alec was leaning on a crutch. Tracy had bandages on her arms and red blotches on her face. Pete's unbeatable legs, and one unbeatable foot, were bandaged. They smiled at Brian. And he knew at once, from their clear, admiring gaze, that they were free. Whether it was the shock of the fire, or the hours they'd spent without honey, something had woken them from their stupor.

Dad pulled up three chairs. The children hobbled over and sat by the bed.

'How are you, Brian?' Tracy sounded almost shy.

'Fine.'

Alec propped his crutch against the chair. 'We brought you these.' He took something out of his dressing-gown pocket and laid it next to Brian's hand. Tracy and Pete did the same.

'The thing is.' Alec coughed. 'You were cleverer than me.'

'And.' Tracy's red face went even redder. 'Everyone thinks you're the coolest boy in school.'

Pete tapped his unbandaged foot on the floor. 'You beat the gardaí to find us. You beat the fire. You're unbeatable.'

Brian stared at the three gold medals. 'Thank you,' he said softly. 'But they belong to someone else. Though I'm not sure they'll fit round her neck.'

The children blinked.

Brian smiled. 'If you hang around, you can give them to her yourself.'

Fifteen minutes later there was a knock. The door opened.

'Where is she?' Brian leaned forward as far as he could.

Alf stood in the doorway, staring at the floor.

'NO!' Brian fell back on the pillow. 'NO!'

Dad laid a hand by his cheek.

Alf looked up. 'She got to dance, Cap'n,' he said softly. 'And she danced for you. But it must have been too much for her poor little body.'

Brian stared at the ceiling. 'And she lied about Mum to make me feel better.' Now he found his tears. They ran down his temples and soaked the pillow.

Alec, Tracy and Pete looked at Dad in bewilderment. He shook his head. They sat in silence.

At last Alf cleared his throat. 'I – um, *we* – were wondering. My girls and I.' He pressed his fists together. 'Apart from me they don't have any male relations. No decent ones anyway. Those drones are a dozy lot. So I – um, *we* – thought p'raps you might consider ...' he rubbed his hands, 'doing us the honour ...' Brian raised his head, 'of becoming their godfather.'

CHAPTER 26

HEROES

The Tully Tattle

19 June

CREEPY CRAWLER CAUGHT ON THE HOP

By Ptolemy Pilps

Tullybun's lousiest lawbreaker is in custody. Gardaí last night arrested a bug-eating thug. In a rare burst of competence, Sergeant Filo Poggarty netted Quincy Queaze after finding the missing schoolchildren in a burnt-out cellar (see yesterday's special evening edition).

'We were later alerted to a suspicious-looking

character in a school uniform seen buying petrol at the garage on Tullbridge Road,' said the man who'd win Tullybun's Favourite Grandpa competition if there was one. 'His car registration was noted by the attendant and we later found the vehicle parked outside Tullbridge Natural History Museum. The suspect had broken in and was examining the butterfly collection. When he unpinned a Red Admiral and popped it into his mouth, we knew we had a nutcase of the first cocoon.'

Queaze, the bees' knees of sleaze, is now awaiting trial on charges of kidnap, arson and perfectly good hearing.

NOTICES

Event: Public unveiling of statue
Date: 17 July
Time: 3 p.m.
Venue: Tullybun Primary,
High Kings of Ireland Street
Please bring: hands to clap, feet to stamp,
streamers and party poppers

It was a tall order. Taller and wider than anything Dad had ever made. But as he was the one who'd ordered it, he didn't complain. For the next four weeks he worked on nothing else, though he was very strict with his hours: two on, two off to play Monopoly with Brian; two on, two off to look through photos of Mum together; two on and the rest off to cook pizza for the classmates who visited Number Six Hercules Drive with invitation upon invitation to the parties they'd planned for when Brian was well.

Which, by the seventeenth of July, he was: or at least well enough to sit in a deckchair on High Street along with Alec, Tracy and Pete and wonder what might be under the canvas-covered lump that Dad was unloading from Drooly McDooly's greengrocer van.

'You must have *some* idea,' said Tracy.

Brian shook his head. 'I've been banned from Dad's workshop since I came home from hospital.'

'Look at the crowd,' said Pete. People were arriving, pushing and shoving to get a good view but leaving a respectful circle around the seated children.

There were mums and dads. There were mums *or* dads. There were grandmas and/or grandpas. There were two hundred and ten aunts, a hundred and ninety-four uncles and four hundred and fifty-two-and-three-quarters neighbours (Mrs Mildew Pritt was wearing high heels). There were three reporters from the local paper. And a patch of pavement was fenced off so that pet rabbits, gerbils and hamsters could come and watch the festivities while nibbling jelly beans. Everyone with any link to the village was there.

Almost. One very important person was missing. Or so it seemed at first.

When the crowd had settled to a whispering fidget, Sergeant Poggarty stood up. 'Ladies and gentlemen,' he boomed, 'children and pets. I'm sure you can't wait to see Tullybun's newest …' Mrs Fontania Mallows tapped him on the shoulder and whispered in his ear … 'er, *only* statue. And here to unveil it, in her last public engagement before she resigns, is the principal of Tullybun Primary. Please give a warm welcome to Mrs Loretta Florris.'

The warm welcome involved whistles, whoops and a burp from Kevin Catwind as the crowd made way for Florrie. She was leaning on the arm of her husband, a thin, pale man seen outdoors so rarely that rumour had it he was nocturnal.

Standing by the statue, the soon-to-be-ex-principal looked saggy and lost. Her helmet of curls had collapsed to a floppy cap. Her nose was Tipp-Ex-free but the permanent marker had lived up to its name. She still sported a faint moustache.

'I am delighted,' she mumbled, looking anything but, 'to unveil this memorial.' She reached forward and pulled off the canvas.

The crowd gasped. People shielded their eyes from the sunlight glinting off the statue. Drooly McDooly, whose head was also glinting impressively, stepped forward. He raised his hand for silence. Then he turned towards the great golden bee with its hunched body, perspex wings and fat back leg. Bending down, he read out the inscription on its gleaming butt.

Brian and Dulcie, a Class Act

The crowd went wild. Hands clapped, feet stamped, party poppers popped and streamers streamed all over Brian O'Bunion.

(When word had got round the village that a twenty-million-year-old bee had alerted Alf and his girls to the fire, reaction had varied. 'Nonsense!' said Fontania Mallows who, as president of the nitting circle, felt a stab of envy on behalf of her rather more timid charges. 'Coo-*wull*,' said Kevin Catwind, who went and had his own ear pierced but let the hole grow over when he couldn't find an earring that talked. 'Whatever,' said Anemia Pickles, blowing a huge spearmint bubble. But everyone agreed that the statue did Brian proud.)

So proud that he couldn't speak. Not that it mattered because Sergeant Poggarty hadn't quite finished. 'I believe,' he said, patting the air for silence, 'Mrs Florris has a few final words for Brian.'

She sniffed. She coughed. She licked her teeth and chewed her cheek. Then she blinked at Brian. 'Thank you,' she whispered, 'for saving my life. And s … ss …'

But she couldn't do it. The 'sorry' died on her faintly moustachioed lips.

There were whistles and whoops and a fake fart from Kevin Catwind as the *very*-soon-to-be-ex-principal was led away by her husband.

And then Miss Emer Pipette stepped forward. In her acceptance speech as the new principal (she'd agreed to come out of retirement), she promised to feed and water the tiny seeds of Tullybun so that they'd bud, blossom and bear much fruit in life, especially strawberries.

And when she asked for volunteers to help her plant small fruits in the school garden, Brian O'Bunion was the first to raise his hand.

Every weekday during the summer holidays he dug, sowed and weeded. Alec, Tracy and Pete tried helping too but gave up when they found that they lacked Brian's green fingers. Much as he enjoyed their company, he was delighted to be left to his other friends: the butterflies, beetles and bees who fluttered and scuttled and buzzed around his work.

On Saturdays he helped to clear up the horror of Quincy's creations. After pouring weedkiller on the magnetic flowers, he worked with other volunteers to convert the house into an insect community centre. In glass cases around the ground-floor room you could watch silkworms eat mulberry leaves and poop shining threads, and butterflies stagger out of cocoons. Fontania Mallows ran her nitting circle there on Tuesdays and started a beetle drive on Thursdays, where the creatures could learn to drive in tiny cars that zoomed round the floor.

And on Sundays Brian helped Alf. They started by moving the poor magnetic bees to a new hive, next door to Brian's forty thousand godchildren. As the weeks went by, and the bees fed on Alf's roses, the iron was washed from their bodies. They began to produce normal honey. Not much, though. Their bottoms remained bulbous and their flight sluggish. So Alf never took honey from their hive and left them to buzz around in peace.

Then came September and secondary school. Brian continued to garden at Tullybun Primary at weekends. Weeding and watering helped him to forget the misery of Maths and the pain of PE. And when he left school it was only natural that Miss Emer Pipette should offer him a permanent job.

Brian adored his work. He loved pruning the raspberry bushes and mowing the calm, comforting lawn. But sometimes, while scraping moss from the rockery or polishing the gnome's hat, he found himself sighing. And if he saw two butterflies scrapping in the air he shivered, too, at the thought of the man he could have become. Then, to reassure himself, he crouched down and picked up a handful of dark, bitter-smelling earth. Opening his palm, he let it fall away through his outspread fingers.

Years passed. Children often came over during break to help him water the redcurrants or pick gooseberries. Not the clever, popular or sporty ones; they were too busy selling their homework or arranging parties or scoring goals. But those who weren't so good at work or friends or football loved to hear him talk about the golden statue, the only spot in Tullybun where no one ever stuck chewing gum. Brian never tired of telling them the story of Tullybun's greatest and tiniest hero.

And when the bell rang at three, he locked up his tools in the tumbledown shed behind the cypress trees and went home to his wife, his children Lily and Tobias, and his old, old dad who still liked to tinker in his workshop at Number Six, Dulcie Drive.